AMARIAS ADVENTURES

QUEST FOR THE SCORPION'S JEWEL

AMY GREEN

D0166981

Published by Warner Press Inc, Anderson, IN 46012
Warner Press and "WP" logo is a trademark of Warner Press Inc.

ISBN: 978-1-59317-432-3

Editors: Karen Rhodes, Robin Fogle
Cover by Curtis D. Corzine
Design and layout: Curtis D. Corzine

Printed in the USA

To my sister Erika,

for loving me no matter what.

CHAPTER I

The city had been too crowded that morning at the hanging. Captain Demetri hated when the people thronged to watch criminals die—making everything noisier and less orderly.

The former captain of Nalatid, a small desert town in District Four of Amarias, had encouraged such spectacles. Even though Demetri did not approve of treating an execution as entertainment, he knew little could be done to stop it. The people didn't understand that death, though necessary at times, was not a game to be played at.

This particular band of marauders had killed four innocent shepherds and stolen their flocks, fleeing to the rocky cliffs for protection. Demetri and his troops had found them within eight hours. They always did.

Now, back in the compound, Demetri set the record book on his desk and opened to the last page. There, listed neatly in columns, were lines of information about the group: its members, last known location, methods, possible escape routes. Beneath each man's name was a description, details about his home and family.

Picking up the pen, Demetri wrote the date and time of the execution in the blank column of the log. The marauders were now dead on paper as well as in reality.

He had kept the record book ever since his promotion to captain the year before, and already its pages were nearly full. Every murderer, bandit, and rebel to set foot in Nalatid had been captured and executed. Sometimes the smugglers evaded his grasp—they weren't as simple-minded as the other criminals—but Demetri was beginning calculations to bring them to justice as well. *Nothing a little planning can't accomplish*, he mused, flipping through the columns of numbers and information in his book.

Captain Demetri had not become a legendary tracker by sheer guesswork. Being a soldier had more to do with strategy and planning than most people realized, and he was good at both. Frighteningly good.

That was what had moved him up the ranks at such a young age. He was barely twenty-one, and yet he commanded an entire outpost. It was not so much the power that Demetri enjoyed. He simply liked to be busy. It was better that way.

As he waited for the ink to dry, Demetri glanced out the small window near his desk. Dusk had long since faded into the shadowy blackness of night, and with the darkness came the welcome cool that brought relief to the scorched desert. Demetri hardly noticed the vague shapes of clay buildings and dusty roads outside his window. He had been in the desert for a long time now, and it had not changed.

A long time.... Demetri blinked. *Five years.* It had been five years since he had lost himself in the Abaktan Desert.

And that means....

Demetri swore under his breath. It was time for another Festival.

He slammed the thick book shut, clenching his teeth. Being angry, he knew, was irrational, but although five years in the desert had darkened his skin and improved his skill with the sword, they could not erase the memories. Nothing could.

No, it was not fair that he had survived when the others in his squad had not. But he was the only one who had to live with the guilt—the memories.

"Sir?" a timid voice from the doorway piped up. It was one of the servants, a young man of about sixteen. *Just like I was five years ago.*

"What do you want?" he growled, more harshly than was necessary.

The servant looked down, too timid to meet the Patrol captain's eyes. "What is it?" Demetri repeated, a bit more patiently.

"There's a man in the courtyard who wants to see you."

"I am busy." It was a lie, but Demetri was hardly in the mood to entertain a visitor to the military compound. "Tell him to come back tomorrow."

"He bears the king's seal on his papers."

Demetri froze, his hand still on the record book, then stood slowly. *The seal...it couldn't be. Not after all this time.* But this was the very time when they would come back.

Five years in the desert. Demetri had hoped they had forgotten about him. That of course was foolish.

The servant, appearing a bit uneasy, added, "He insists on seeing you."

Of course he does. Demetri forced his face into the blank, stoic mask he wore around the troops and nodded at the servant. "I will be there shortly."

Demetri sank back into his chair, his mind whirling as frantically as a desert storm. He had to meet with this stranger sent from the king. There was no way to avoid it. He did not know who the man would be, but he knew why he was there.

He fought for composure, for the emotionless objectivity that made him the perfect Patrol captain. His duty was to the king, and he would fulfill that duty. No matter what it cost.

Demetri moved quickly and silently down the halls of the compound, ignoring the salutes of the Patrol members on watch. Before he entered the courtyard, he peered out from a crack in the door.

There, over by the compound gate. A man, stooped slightly with age and dressed in a simple dark robe, was staring at the doorway where Demetri stood, almost as if he were watching him. It was hard to make out his features, since he stood a distance away from the fire that warmed the Patrol members on guard duty, but Demetri knew it was one of them. One of the Riders.

Demetri did not pause to think about the man further, knowing if he did he might turn back. Resolutely he strode out into the courtyard, letting the black cape that indicated his rank billow behind him in the desert wind.

"What are you doing in my city?" he demanded, drawing

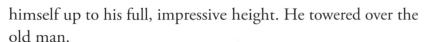

himself up to his full, impressive height. He towered over the old man.

Instead of responding, the old man laughed. Demetri was reminded of an echo in a cavern—the sound, hollow and empty. "*Your* city? Is that what you think?"

Demetri didn't respond. Any response would be taken as a sign of weakness.

"You think you are important, boy?" the old man continued. "You and I—we are nothing but grains of sand, insignificant parts of a greater whole." Before Demetri could respond, the man pulled something from beneath his shapeless cloak and held it up.

Glinting in the dim light from the nearby fire was a golden medallion, inscribed with the symbol of King Selen of Amarias.

Demetri had seen a medallion like it only once before in his life, exactly five years before, when he watched the other members of his squad die before his very eyes. *They should have killed me too.*

But he knew why they had not. They knew that someday he would be of use to them. That day had come.

Feeling like every step was forced, Demetri escorted the old man to his quarters and dismissed the guards outside. Silence lasted a moment, and Demetri knew he was being studied. The old man's pale eyes were watching him in the dim candlelight.

Demetri was the first to break the silence. "Who are you?"

"You may call me Aleric, Captain. You made an agreement five years ago. I am here to collect."

Demetri had thought he was prepared to hear these words, ones he had expected the moment the servant had mentioned the seal. Still, he felt the color drain from his face.

"Do I need to remind you," Aleric asked casually, "what will happen if you refuse?"

"No," Demetri said. "If I refuse, you will kill my brother. I once failed those who depended on me. It will never happen again."

For a brief moment Aleric paused, stroking his thin beard. "I often wondered why the last Chief Rider didn't kill you when he had the chance. Perhaps I know now. You love your brother, don't you?"

Demetri did not care to speak of his brother anymore. "What do you want from me?" he asked, drilling Aleric with a cold stare.

"You know that the Festival is tomorrow."

Demetri's expression never changed. He made sure of it. "Yes."

"The Youth Guard will be sent out. One squad will be coming through your district on the way to Da'armos." Aleric's tone remained flat, lifeless. "You are to make sure they do not arrive."

Five years in the desert had taught Demetri more than strategy: it had taught him the importance of following orders, whether he liked them or not. And now his brother's life was at stake. "I will not fail you," he promised, never flinching.

"See that you don't," Aleric said. "They are clever ones, you know. Chosen from all the districts of Amarias: the bravest, strongest, most principled and intelligent...."

"I know," Demetri interrupted, looking away. "Believe me, I know."

"That's right," Aleric said. "I had forgotten. You were once in the Guard, correct? At the last Festival commissioning, five years ago?"

Demetri clenched his jaw. He knew Aleric had not forgotten. *He merely wants me to remember. But I will not.*

"You never answered my question. Who are you?" he asked abruptly. "I know your name is Aleric, and that you work for the king, but I know nothing else about you."

"You know nothing about the Guard Riders?" Aleric pressed, staring at him again. "I would think a military leader such as yourself would have found out more. Especially a military leader with your…background."

He was right, of course, but Demetri did not admit it. He wanted to hear from Aleric himself. "I only know that the Riders were the ones who killed the others in my squad."

"There is little else to know," Aleric replied with a shrug. "We cannot let the Youth Guard members live. Occasionally the king will order that one member of a squad be allowed to succeed, to keep the people happy, but that is the exception, not the rule."

"And sometimes, a few escape, never to be heard from again," Demetri added, "or turn to the king's side, like me."

Aleric nodded. "But most Youth Guard die before they become old enough to challenge the king—to challenge us."

None of the people knew this, of course. They might complain about King Selen's high taxes, or how he drafted their sons into his army, but they did not know that Guard

Riders like Aleric killed the Youth Guard at the king's order. All of the people believed the lie that the children who died were heroes, perishing in a noble quest to help their country. And, as long as they did not know the truth, peace reigned in Amarias.

Aleric half-lowered his eyes, squinting intently at Demetri. "And I trust you will *remain* loyal to the king, or your brother will be the one to pay the price this time."

My brother. Demetri hadn't seen him for five years, since he had left home.

"I am the captain of the Guard Riders," Aleric continued. "All others are under my authority, and I, in turn, am under the authority of the king." The implied threat was clear in Aleric's words and his eyes—*you don't dare defy me, boy.*

"Will I report to you when they are dead?" Demetri asked. He left his real question unspoken: *And then will you leave me in peace?*

"In a manner of speaking."

Demetri waited for Aleric to explain, but he merely reached into a pocket in his cloak and withdrew a medallion, identical to the one he had shown Demetri earlier. "Wear it with pride," he said. "It is carried by all Guard Riders. You may give your other medallion to me."

Demetri's hand went automatically to his neck. "How did you...?"

Aleric's pale eyes chilled Demetri, even in the dry desert heat. "I have ways of knowing that you would never understand."

Almost without realizing he was doing it, Demetri

unfastened the silver chain from around his neck and handed his medallion to Aleric, who held it up, examining the red dragon engraved in the center. "Your family crest," he observed. "I would have thought you would want to forget everything from your past."

"Not everything," Demetri said without emotion. He placed the Guard Rider medallion around his neck and slipped it under his uniform. It felt hot against his skin.

"I will return it to you when your task is complete," Aleric said, the dragon medallion disappearing into the dark folds of his robe. "You must wear the symbol of the Guard Rider at all times. I will know if you take it off, and I will take it as a sign of treachery."

Demetri frowned. "Why is it so important?"

Aleric answered the question with one of his own. "Do you dream often, Captain?"

The smell of incense burning...foreign shouts and the clang of swords...that endless scream.... Demetri shook his head. "No." *I do not have dreams anymore. Only nightmares.*

"You will now. And that is how I will know you have accomplished your task." Instead of explaining, Aleric chuckled dryly. "Ironic, isn't it? What you are being asked to do? To kill Youth Guard members when you yourself once belonged to the Guard."

Demetri smiled slightly, noticing the look of surprise on the old man's face. It was not the reaction he was expecting. But Demetri knew his duty, and he would do it, for his brother's sake. "*J'abbet ses mitren, oldrivar lakita ses omidreden.*"

"Excuse me?"

"A Da'armon proverb I've learned during my years along the border," Demetri replied. "It translates roughly to, 'If you release the wind, you must be prepared to reap the whirlwind.'"

Now Aleric nodded, looking pleased. "You mean, of course, that actions have consequences."

"Yes," Demetri said. "I made a choice years ago—ally myself with the king to save my family. I released the wind. Now I have no choice. The squad will not leave my territory alive. You will give me more details when the time comes?"

Aleric nodded. "They will be followed closely, of course. You will know when they come through Nalatid."

"I will make sure they are dead. And no one will be able to stop me."

"Oh? Not even God?" Though Aleric asked it casually, Demetri could see a spark of interest in his eyes. This man, like Demetri himself, loved to analyze others.

He is welcome to this information. Demetri laughed, a hard, bitter laugh, and turned to face him. "Many of the desert people cling to their old superstitions. I know some here who still believe in God. I do not."

From the look on Aleric's face, it was a satisfactory answer. "Yes," he said, shrugging. "Many prefer to deny the existence of the Enemy. The main thing is that both you and I will fight to the end. Isn't that right?"

Now it was Demetri's turn to shrug. He turned to face the window, hoping Aleric would leave. *The man has long overstayed his welcome.* "If you say so."

Despite what Aleric said, Demetri knew there was no God. There couldn't be. Not with all the evil he had seen.

"Do you believe you made the right choice five years ago, Captain, knowing what you do now?"

Demetri paused for a second, but did not turn to face Aleric. "No one can gather back the wind once it is released, Aleric." His voice was quiet, measured, but it had a hollow emptiness that seemed to make it echo dully through the room. "All that matters now is being the one left standing when the whirlwind clears."

When Demetri finally turned around, Aleric was gone. He hadn't even heard the old man slip through the door.

Demetri lowered himself silently into his chair, opening up the record book. He had done what was necessary. His brother's life—that was what mattered.

But is it right? Demetri buried the thought, sent it back with the other memories and beliefs he never wanted to see again.

Then he began to write, recording everything he knew about the Guard, about Aleric, about his mission. Usually, recording information was a way for him to relax before going to sleep, but not tonight. Tonight he would find no peace.

He was in the middle of a list when a knock at the door interrupted his thoughts. "What is it?" he asked, turning around wearily.

This time there was no servant boy in the doorway. Instead, a frightened-looking Patrol member stood at stiff attention. "Report," Demetri demanded. *There must be trouble.*

The Patrol member's hand trembled as he saluted. "My partner and I were guarding the city gate," he began, his words bumping into each other like a train of clumsy camels. "An old man came...."

An old man. Demetri groaned inwardly. *What has Aleric done?*

"We stopped him, it being after curfew and all," the Patrol member babbled, his eyes wide. "He told us he was on the king's business, but my partner didn't believe him.... "

"Get to the point," Demetri snapped. "What happened?"

"The old man stabbed him," the Patrol member said, his face registering complete shock. "Right there before my eyes. I swear, we only asked him to prove his papers weren't forged...."

But Demetri had stopped listening. *What kind of a man is this?* he wondered, fingering the medallion. Demetri knew without a doubt that the Patrol member's death had been intended as a warning for him.

A warning well taken. Demetri had survived the whirlwind five years before; he would survive now. The Youth Guard members would die.

Demetri turned back to the book of records and continued to write. The Patrol member's report had given him even more information to record.

"Aren't you going to do something about the old man?" the Patrol member demanded. "What about the law?"

"The old man *is* the law in the kingdom of Amarias," Demetri said shortly. He saw the confusion in the Patrol member's eyes, but offered no further explanation. "You are dismissed."

Demetri stayed up until midnight writing, thinking, and planning. As he blew out the candle, he took one last glance out the window. And for the first time, looking into the desert night, he felt fear.

CHAPTER 2

The empty inn was littered with a graveyard of empty soup bowls, chicken bones, and overturned chairs, creating eerie shadows in the near darkness. Only a little heat came from the dying embers in the fireplace, and curls of smoke escaped from the cracked brickwork. Jesse shivered, trying to finish his chores quickly so he could go to sleep like everyone else.

I hate the Festival, he decided, scrubbing furiously at a soup stain on Aunt Dara's best tablecloth, the one they had brought out from storage to accommodate the extra guests. All of the travelers coming home from the Festival were louder, sweatier, and more irritable than normal, and that didn't put Jesse in a good mood.

It's not really the Festival, Jesse thought, giving the table an especially hard swipe. *It's the fact that Uncle Tristan and Aunt Dara wouldn't let me* go *to the Festival.*

Terenid, the capital city of Amarias, was only a few hours' journey away from the village of Mir. Jesse had gone there five years before for the last Festival, when he was ten. *But that was when Mother and Father were still here.*

Jesse hated busy nights at the inn. There was too much noise, and there always seemed to be a mean-spirited traveler who mocked Jesse's crippled left leg. *"Hey, boy! Hurry that stump of yours along. I'm hungry."* Though he had learned long ago to ignore the taunts, they still stung.

Now, with all the guests asleep upstairs and Uncle Tristan and Aunt Dara away in their room, at least Jesse had a few hours of quiet. That was the only thing he enjoyed about cleaning the inn every night. In the empty room, he was free to let his mind wander, taking him to the better times of the past or the possible adventures of the future.

Tonight, though, he could only think of his aching leg and empty stomach. *Just make it through the night,* he thought wearily. *That's all that matters.*

His mother would tell him to focus on positive thoughts, Jesse knew. *But Mother is gone. She's the one who left me here with Uncle Tristan and Aunt Dara in the first place.*

He had heard people talking about how good and kind Tristan and Dara were for taking in their crippled nephew after his parents disappeared—listened as the village priest practically assured them the generous deed would get them into heaven.

That was what Jesse hated most—no one knew what his aunt and uncle were really like. They just saw a fat, jovial innkeeper and his sweet, pale wife who always had a good tale to tell and a warm bowl of soup on the fire.

Jesse's father had known. That's why, even though they lived on a farm on the other side of Mir, they rarely visited Uncle Tristan and Aunt Dara. "They're not bad people, Son," he had always said when Jesse asked why. "They just have their priorities wrong."

A sharp knock broke into his thoughts, and Jesse jumped, nearly dropping a plate. *Another guest?* He started to move toward the door, then stopped. *But it's after curfew!*

Once the sun went down, citizens of Amarias were forbidden to leave their homes. No one wandered the streets, not even in the small village of Mir, or they could be arrested, even killed, by the king's Patrol.

The knock came again, louder this time. Jesse glanced toward his uncle's room on the far side of the hall, unsure of what to do.

It could be a bandit, or perhaps a member of the Rebellion. Then Jesse shook his head at his foolishness. *No lawbreaker would come to an inn for the night. Most likely it's a traveler from another land who doesn't know of the law.*

Jesse grabbed the lone candle from the fireplace mantle, holding it out like a magic charm against whatever was behind the door. He couldn't stop his hand from trembling as he eased the door open a crack.

The harsh wind, cold for March, nearly blew out the flame before Jesse shielded it. Two cloaked figures huddled together on the porch of the inn. "We need a place to stay," the taller one said. His tone of voice left no room for questions.

Jesse opened the door wider and took a closer look. *They don't* seem *dangerous.* One was a tall young man, probably a few years older than Jesse. He stood straight and tall, and the wheat blond hair, nearly white, that stuck out from his hood shone in the moonlight. The other, a slight figure, was little more than a girl, the cold creating two red blotches on her pale cheeks.

"Can you pay?" Jesse asked automatically. That was always Uncle Tristan's first concern.

"Yes," the girl said, digging around in the pouch she carried, "and well too." Her voice had a strange, lilting quality to it, an accent Jesse had heard from travelers from District Three.

Then Jesse noticed something else. The girl's small hand was holding out a golden sceptre coin. Jesse was used to being paid only in crownes. Even more often, travelers would pay in kind, giving his uncle a chicken or a basket of apples in exchange for a room. Times were hard, and few had enough money for the luxuries of travel. *Where did these two get such wealth?*

Jesse knew that would not be a proper question to ask a guest. "May I see your papers?" he asked instead.

Every good citizen of Amarias carried their identification papers with them at all times. The papers listed the name, occupation, and legal status of each person, distinguishing them from escaped criminals, street urchins, spies, and other ruffians. All inns in the country registered each person who stayed with them.

So Jesse drew back in surprise when the tall stranger said, "No."

That was all. Just a simple "no," without explanation.

Jesse knew he should shut the door immediately, but he was curious. "Are you slaves?" he guessed. "Run away from your master?" The Festival, with its teeming crowds and boisterous parade, would be an ideal time for an escape.

No response, so Jesse continued, "Or lovers, perhaps, running away to marry without your families' permission?"

That at least got a reaction. The girl scoffed loudly. "Never!" she declared, glaring up at the tall young man.

"Then why are you out after curfew, with no identification?"

"That does not concern you," the tall stranger said, his tone flat and even. "All we ask is that you allow us to stay at this inn."

"I can't. It's the law."

"Hang the law!" the girl said, stepping forward and grabbing Jesse's arm. This close, he could see dark eyes burning in her small, pretty face. "Our friend is hurt!"

Jesse wrenched away in alarm, then realized what the girl had said. "There's another one of you?"

The girl nodded, then stepped aside. Behind them was the slumped form of a young man. Jesse could hear his soft moaning, even over the bitter wind.

"He might die if he can't get inside," the tall stranger said. "Will you let us in?" They stood there, shivering in the cold, waiting for Jesse to answer.

Without meaning to, Jesse remembered a story the village priest had once told. He and his family had never been much for religion—most priests and their followers were hypocrites and liars—but Jesse remembered this story.

It was about a man and a woman, both poor, who stumbled

into a crowded town, looking for a place to stay. The woman was about to have a baby, but everyone turned them away.

Jesse remembered asking the priest what the point was to the story. He had coughed, looked away, and then finally said he didn't know.

Now Jesse thought he could guess. The story was about the ones who had closed their doors on the couple. Jesse's father disliked talk of God, but he always said people had a responsibility to help each other when they could. Although Jesse's parents barely had enough left after taxes to survive on, they always found a way to visit the sick, give some of their rations to a neighbor in need, or let a passing beggar spend the night.

"All right," Jesse said, pulling the door open. "Bring him in."

"What's going on?" a familiar voice bellowed, much too loudly for the quiet night.

Jesse didn't bother to turn around, knowing who the voice belonged to. "More travelers, Uncle Tristan," he said instead. How one so large could manage to sneak up on him, Jesse was never sure.

Uncle Tristan lumbered forward, shoving Jesse aside to get to the door. "Why are you out after curfew?" he demanded, loud enough to disturb the guests in the room above them. "Who are you? Where are your papers?"

"We can't show them to you," the tall stranger responded, never flinching.

Even in the dim candlelight, Jesse could see the suspicion in his uncle's eyes. "You mean you don't have any."

"No, he means exactly what he said," the girl put in, crossing her arms in defiance. "We can't show them to you."

"Enough, Rae," the other said, frowning.

"Get away from here," Uncle Tristan said, shaking his fat fist at them. "We don't take your kind at this inn."

"But, Uncle," Jesse protested, "they have a sick friend with them."

"Can't be helped," Uncle Tristan growled. "If we let in guests without papers, the Patrol will find out, and we get thrown out on the streets." He shook Jesse by the shoulder. "Is that what you want, boy? To be homeless like you should have been when your parents left you?"

Without realizing it, Jesse's hands tightened into fists. *Don't say anything,* he said, hoping the darkness would hide the expression on his face. *Don't let him know it upsets you.*

Jesse didn't believe what everyone else said, that his parents had left for District Four to find work, and left him because they couldn't feed a third mouth. What they meant—Jesse knew from the way that they glanced down at his crippled leg—was that his parents hadn't been able to support a boy who couldn't do his share of the work.

Nearly a year had passed, and no news had come from his parents. *Maybe it would be better if they were dead. At least then I would stop hoping they will come back.*

"We have to tell them, Silas," the girl, Rae, said in a low voice, glancing at Jesse briefly before turning back to him.

"No," Silas said, shaking his head. "We can't be sure we can trust them."

They can't trust us?

Uncle Tristan started to shut the door, but Jesse stepped over the threshold, blocking it. "I don't understand," he said, watching the strangers carefully.

Rae threw her cloak to the side, letting it blow in the wind, and rolled up the loose sleeve of her dress. There, tattooed on her shoulder, was the symbol of Amarias. The familiar *A*, enclosed in a broken circle, could mean only one thing.

"You're Youth Guard members," Jesse said, his eyes wide in awe. *The most famous troops of all of the land…here, at our inn!*

"Yes," Rae said, nodding sharply. "We didn't want to show you our papers because…" She glanced around at the shadows around the inn. "Enemies of the king are everywhere."

"This is…that is, I…." Uncle Tristan's round face contorted as he stuttered. "Please, excuse my behavior," he said, giving a quick bow. "I did not know. That is, you did not say."

"Please," Silas said, holding up a hand to stop his blustering. "We just need a place to stay. We already put our horses in your stable."

Normally, Uncle Tristan would be outraged that strangers broke into one of his buildings, but he didn't even seem to notice. "I'll get my best room ready," he said, hurrying away.

Jesse knew that he would throw out any of his guests to accommodate the Youth Guard members, but Rae stopped him. "No. We don't want anyone to know we are here. Just give us some food and let us sleep in the hall. We'll leave at dawn."

Uncle Tristan bowed again and scurried off to the kitchen, forgetting, in his confusion, to give Jesse any orders.

The two Youth Guard members leaned over their fallen friend. "How bad is the sickness?" Jesse asked, trying to see over Silas' shoulder. The village hermit, Kayne, had taught him a few things about treating fevers, although he did not have the old man's natural gift for identifying healing herbs.

"He's not sick," Silas said, easing the man up. "He was shot with an arrow."

"We think it was one of the Rebellion, sent to assassinate us," Rae added flatly.

Just hearing the name made Jesse shudder. Everyone knew of the secret group that worked to undermine the king, but few dared to speak their name out loud.

Silas and Rae lifted the body with what seemed to be little effort. Jesse opened the door for them, looking on as they laid the man down on the floor by the fireplace.

Jesse brought the candle closer, getting a good look at the sick stranger. He was young, Jesse knew, since Youth Guard members were between the ages of fourteen and eighteen. His dark brown hair was matted to his head with sweat. Even though his burly form reminded Jesse of a mountain bear, his arms hung limply at his side.

"No," the young man groaned quietly. Jesse jumped. "He never going up me had to there disappear."

"It's getting worse," Rae whispered. She slumped into a chair, still watching her friend.

Silas' mind appeared to be somewhere else. "You shouldn't have told them, Rae," he said, staring into the ashes of the fire.

"I had to!" she protested. "Parvel might have died because of you and your foolish caution."

"My caution may save all of our lives," Silas snapped. "There is a reason why only eleven Guard members out of hundreds have come back alive with their mission completed."

Even though he forced himself not to move, Jesse flinched inwardly. Of course, he knew that most of the Youth Guard died or disappeared. It was the nature of the difficult missions they attempted. This year, though, he had a personal interest in the statistic. His childhood friend, Eli, was in this year's Youth Guard. Only one hundred were chosen, the best of the kingdom, and he had been one of them.

Perhaps Eli will be the twelfth to live and return to Mir, a hero. Although the thought was comforting, Jesse couldn't help but feel a twinge of jealousy. Eli was everything a Youth Guard member should be—tall, strong, and darkly handsome. Jesse hadn't even attended the muster. *As if the Guard would want a cripple like me anyway.*

Although he knew he should be helping his uncle prepare food, or perhaps getting a spare blanket for the injured man, Jesse couldn't force himself to leave. The young man—the others had called him Parvel—twitched and contorted in pain, his eyes still closed.

This was not like any arrow wound Jesse had ever seen. "Is he…" Jesse paused, not wanting to ask it. "Is he going to die?"

"I don't know," Rae said, seeming to shrink in the chair, her confident air gone. "It makes no sense. It wasn't a bad wound. The arrow hit his arm."

"The archer had poor aim," Silas added.

"What happened to him?" Jesse asked.

Silas held up a longbow that Jesse had not noticed in the darkness. "I don't have poor aim."

Without thinking, Jesse edged away from Silas and toward Parvel. He looked at the young man's sweaty face. "This is not an ordinary sickness," Jesse declared, turning to Rae and Silas. "Your friend needs help—and soon."

"Thank you for that enlightening information," Rae shot back. "Maybe we should risk our lives to travel back to the capital on the main roads to get a doctor."

"I know someone who can help you," Jesse said, ignoring her rude tone. "He's close by. It wouldn't be dangerous." Kayne lived deep in the thickets of the woods behind the inn, where no Patrol member ever went.

"You are sure?" This from Silas, who was staring intently at Jesse, as if he could read his mind.

"Yes."

Silas glanced again at Parvel's limp form. He moaned again, and that seemed to settle the matter for Silas. "All right," he said, standing. "Let's go."

CHAPTER 3

Even though Rae and Silas were carrying Parvel, Jesse had a hard time keeping up with the two Youth Guard members as they made their way through the dark woods. Jesse leaned heavily on his good leg, trying to ignore the contorted shadows of tree branches that kept the pale moonlight from lighting the path.

Uncle Tristan hadn't put forth a single objection to Jesse leading the way to Kayne's cabin, especially not after Rae tossed him a sceptre coin. Jesse guessed Uncle Tristan would have sold him to them as a slave for that amount of money.

Through the trees, Jesse saw the familiar outline of Kayne's cabin. There was no road to it—hardly anyone came to visit the old man—but Jesse had worn a little path in the moss and grass of the forest. "We're here," he announced, pointing.

"That's it?" Rae said flatly, staring at it.

Jesse knew why. Kayne's cabin—most called it a shack—looked like it could barely stand up. One side leaned against the twisted brush of the pine tree beside it, and the roof looked like a heap of scrap lumber. Jesse had offered to help Kayne repair it many times, but his offers were always met with gruff refusal. Everyone in Mir gossiped about it, wondering why a gifted carpenter like Kayne would choose to live in such a rundown shack.

Jesse nodded. "A friend of mine lives here. He'll know how to help Parvel."

Silas moved toward the door, but Rae remained firmly where she was, making Silas jerk to a sudden halt. "How do we know this isn't a trap?" she demanded.

"Excellent point," Jesse said calmly, knocking on the door. "You should probably stay here in the forest until Parvel dies and the two of you get ripped apart by wild beasts."

No one came to the door. Jesse tried again.

This time, a loud, raspy voice from inside the shack hollered, loud enough to call in any Patrol within several miles, "Go away! Don't you know it's past curfew?"

"Kayne, it's Jesse."

Another pause, and then the familiar sound of Kayne's shuffling footsteps. The door eased open on shaky hinges, and Kayne, holding a candle, peered out. "What is it?" he demanded, his wrinkled, mottled face squinting in annoyance.

"There's been a terrible accident," Jesse said, not sure how else to explain. He gestured to Parvel. "He's badly hurt."

For a moment, Kayne's old eyes studied the three strangers with a surprising sharpness. Then he opened the door wider and turned to go inside. "Always bringing trouble to me, aren't you, Jesse?" he muttered. "Wish you could just stay at that hovel of an inn and be peaceable like everyone else in this rotten town."

Jesse didn't let Kayne's words bother him. It was just his way. Everyone else in Mir called him a crazy old hermit, since he rarely ventured out of his old cabin. "An outcast by choice," Kayne always said.

Maybe that's why I get along with him so well.

The inside of Kayne's shack was as clean and orderly as the outside was dilapidated. What's more, each piece of furniture, though simple, showed the elegant construction of a master carpenter.

Rae and Silas, however, didn't appear to be studying Kayne's benches or tables. Instead, they laid Parvel down on a rug in the middle of the floor. The impact made him jerk about, kicking Rae's leg with enough force to make her wince.

Kayne was already going to the hand-carved cabinet that held his medical supplies. He was not an official doctor— outside of the main cities, there were very few—but he knew more about healing herbs than anyone else in Mir. "That's the only reason those fools don't run me out of town," he always said.

"Get more candles," Kayne ordered Jesse. "I'll need some light."

Jesse scrambled through the kitchen and Kayne's small bedchamber, taking all that he could find. When he returned, Kayne was kneeling beside Parvel.

"What kind of accident?" he barked.

Jesse thought about Parvel's strange behavior as he fumbled to light the candles. "We're…we're not sure."

Kayne just grunted, as if that was the response he expected. "This young fellow is burning up with fever."

Jesse stepped closer. In the flickering light of the candles, he could see that Parvel's face was red and shiny with sweat, tightening every few seconds in spasms of pain.

Kayne laid a gnarled hand on Parvel's forehead, listened to his heart rate, and pried open his eyes to examine them.

At this last intrusion, Parvel jerked violently. "Don't want to need a forever after once had! What happened? No finding what living best in guards."

Kayne stiffened visibly at the outburst, then raised his head. "You," he said, pointing to Silas, "bring a bucket of cool water from the well outside the kitchen. He needs a wet cloth."

Silas hadn't even waited to hear the rest of the instructions. The front door slammed shut as he ran outside.

"Jesse, get the dispur leaves I use for poultices," he continued. "As many as I have. And a rag."

Jesse yanked aside the curtain that separated the kitchen from the rest of the shack and limped over to the hand-carved cabinet. The leaves were in a canister on the top shelf. Next to it were the stone mortar and pestle Kayne used to grind up the herbs and roots. There was a neat stack of clean rags in the left drawer. For all of the disorganization of the kitchen—dirty dishes were scattered everywhere—Kayne had enough common sense to keep his medical supplies organized.

"Here," Jesse called, bursting back into the room and setting the objects on the hard-packed dirt floor. The arrow was gone from Parvel's arm, and some blood had soaked into the rug. Jesse looked away.

Now Kayne turned to Rae, who was standing

uncomfortably to the side, looking anxious. "You going to tell me what happened to this boy?"

Rae started to speak, then stopped.

Kayne sighed loudly, tearing up the dispur leaves and pounding them rhythmically. "From the looks of things, it ain't a complicated story. Might as well get it out, or there's not much I can do."

"He was shot," Rae said, gesturing to the wound in Parvel's arm. "With a crossbow. I'm sure you can see that."

"Don't be rude," Jesse snapped. "He's just trying to help."

"Well," Kayne said, hands still moving busily, "who was this mysterious archer and why was he shooting at you?"

"We don't know," Rae said. "The Rebellion, maybe. Is Parvel going to be all right?"

"Can't make any promises, 'cept one: I'll do what I can."

Silas rushed in, sloshing water from the bucket on the floor. Kayne soaked the rag with water. After wringing it, he placed the cloth on Parvel's feverish forehead, then went back to pounding the dispur leaves.

It was a frightening thing, staring at Parvel in the dim torchlight. He was curled up like a small child, pain tightening his face and sending him into occasional spasms.

"He's a good person," Rae said quietly, almost to herself. "Always smiling, even during the hardest days of training. He was always talking about God, always looking out for others. I laughed at him for it."

She paused, and Jesse couldn't think of anything to say. "The man with the crossbow was aiming for me, but Parvel knocked me away."

"Oh," Jesse said lamely, looking down. "I'm sorry."

"Don't be," she snapped, turning away, as if realizing she had sounded like a human being for a few moments.

Kayne scooped out the dispur leaves, now a thick, dark, poultice, and smeared it on Parvel's arm by the wound. Parvel jerked, eyes still tightly closed.

"That should help bring the fever down," he said grimly, "but I've seen enough to know that we're dealing with something more…complicated, you might say."

"What?" Silas asked, kneeling beside Parvel.

"No," Parvel moaned again. "Can't be justice only have brother in."

"The symptoms look an awful lot like a deadly poison, extracted from the tarroot plant. Hunters in the Black Woods—"

"— tip their arrows with it," Rae finished, her voice devoid of any expression. "Only to shoot wolves and other predators, of course. It's too deadly to use on game that humans would eat later. I should have guessed."

For a moment, Kayne looked at Rae quizzically. "That's where you're from, then?" he asked. "The Black Woods in District Three."

Rae just nodded, not offering any more information.

"The person who shot your friend," Kayne continued, staring at the gash in Parvel's arm. "Why would he want to poison him?"

"Are you a doctor or a Patrol member?" Rae shot back.

"Neither," Kayne said, meeting her hostile gaze, "but I am a law-abiding man, and I want to know if I'm harboring criminals or fugitives."

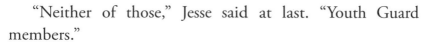

"Neither of those," Jesse said at last. "Youth Guard members."

Rae gave him a cutting glare, but Silas never looked away from Kayne. "It's true," he admitted. "We came from the Festival just this morning, to begin our mission. That's why it's so important that Parvel recovers."

"Guard members, eh?" Kayne mused, leaning back against the wall. "Huh. Ought to have gotten out the fine china."

"He won't tell anyone," Jesse promised Silas and Rae. Of everyone he knew, Kayne was the best at keeping secrets.

"I'm no scholar," Kayne said, eyes still fixed on Silas and Rae. "Jesse here does all of my readin' and writin' for me, but I know how to count. There's three of you. Don't Youth Guard squads have four?"

"Yes," Silas said, eyebrows locked into two hard, straight lines. "Our fourth member—a girl named Aleiah—died during the training. One night, she didn't come back from our runs. They found her dead of exhaustion along the route."

Jesse said nothing, because there was nothing to say. *If the Youth Guard training is so harsh, what are the missions like?*

"For almost until justice," Parvel babbled. "Only red." The strings of nonsense were less anguished now, and Jesse hoped that meant his pain was lessening.

Or maybe it means he's slowly dying.

"Will he live?" Rae asked bluntly.

"Maybe," Kayne said. "So long as we can keep the fever at bay until morning. Then I can go into the woods by the mountain, get some knob willow bark. Far as I know, that's the only antidote."

"Don't you keep any here?" Rae demanded.

"This isn't District Two," Jesse said, defending Kayne. "There are no tarroot plants here, and no need to keep the antidote in stock."

Silas nodded. "Then we'll just have to wait."

"No," Jesse said quietly. All of them looked up. "No," he said, louder this time. "We need to do something now!"

"Don't you move, boy," Kayne commanded, standing slowly. "No one's goin' anywhere. It's after curfew, and you know the law as well as I do."

"The law was made to protect us from thieves and murderers," Jesse said, "not to keep us from helping someone in need."

Even as he said it, Jesse wondered if it was true. His father and even his uncle had complained many times that the curfew wasn't meant to protect the people; it was meant to be one more way to control them. *But surely even the king wouldn't want one of his Youth Guard members to die.*

Rae shook her head impatiently. "There are bound to be Patrol members wandering the streets, even in this small village. The night after the Festival is a good time for thieves. They will attack first and ask questions later." She glanced down at Jesse's leg. "And I don't think you can outrun them."

"But…" Jesse protested.

"No," Kayne said, cutting him off. "Don't like riskin' more than one life at a time." He nodded at Parvel. "And since he got here first, you're just gonna have to wait in line."

"Parvel is strong. He'll be fine," Silas said in a calming voice.

Jesse pretended to listen to him and nodded. "You're right." The words sounded forced and hollow, even to him. "I suppose there's nothing more we can do."

But there *was* something he could do, and Jesse knew it. He bent down and touched the cloth on Parvel's forehead. "Warm already. I'll draw some fresh water."

Picking up the bucket—still half full—Jesse hurried out the front door. No one called out after him, so he set the bucket down beside the cabin wall. They would discover where he had gone soon enough, when he didn't return.

It was a crazy idea, Jesse knew—risking his life for a complete stranger. But every time he looked at Parvel's helpless body, he remembered his parents. Whatever had happened to them, someone could have stopped it. But they chose not to.

I will not let an innocent person die, Jesse vowed, hurrying through the dark woods. *Not if I can do something about it.*

GHAPTER 4

Jesse pressed himself against the stone wall of the grain mill, trying not to move. He had run—or, at least, limped quickly—all the way across the village. Now his breath came in short, tired bursts, and he knew he had to wait until his aching lungs had time to recover before he went farther.

Just beyond the mill was a bonfire where three large Patrol members stood, talking and laughing in low tones. Just beyond them was a stone bridge, spanning the dark waters of the Dell River. And just beyond the river was a grove of trees that fringed the cliffs of the Suspicion Mountains.

The trees that contained the power to save Parvel.

I have to get over there, Jesse knew. *But how?*

His first thought was that he should step out and declare his reason for being out after curfew. *Surely they wouldn't let an innocent man die.*

A second later, the problems with this solution flooded his mind. Patrol members were not known for their compassion, or even their intelligence. They were valued for their brute strength and blind loyalty, sworn to enforce the commands of the king. Jesse could not count on their help, no matter what the circumstances.

And they probably wouldn't believe me anyway. In these hard times it was not uncommon for young boys to steal what they could not afford to buy. Surely these thieves, when caught, made wild excuses.

No, he would have to think of a different plan.

He looked at the river. It was not at flood stage yet, but the water moved by quickly, and Jesse knew it would at least be up to his chest in the middle. *I can't wade across. It would make too much noise.*

A quick glance back at the bridge showed him that while the road was securely blocked, he could reach the bridge itself without being seen. The bonfire was a distance away from the bridge, and if he was careful to be quiet, he could sneak over without any of them noticing. *But if one of the guards turns his head and sees me walking across....* On the bridge, silhouetted starkly against the moonlight, there would be no place to hide.

Then Jesse remembered all the times he and Eli had played by the river when they were young. He grinned to himself. *Maybe I don't need to go* over *the bridge after all.*

The spongy moss on the riverbank muffled Jesse's movements as he crept toward the bridge, ready at any moment to drop and flatten himself to the ground if one of the Patrol members looked his way.

They were huddled around the large bonfire. Their voices rose and fell; once he reached the bridge Jesse was close enough to hear every word of the exaggerated stories they told each other.

He did not take the time to listen, though. Instead, he studied the underside of the Dell River bridge. Huge, thick pillars supported its weight, and between these, nearly touching the stone underside of the bridge, wooden supports ran from one side of the bridge to the other, further strengthening the structure.

Jesse knew the supports would hold him. They were solid enough to bear the weight of a caravan of merchants on horseback with carts and wagons. For a hundred years they had stood guard under the bridge, solidly doing their duty without a moment's rest. No, there was no question about the beams' strength.

It was his own that worried him.

Ever since the accident had left him crippled in one leg, Jesse had not run about as in the old days. He knew he was much weaker than the young boy who had once played Sea Serpent in the river.

Pretend that's what you're doing now, Jesse thought, forcing himself to breathe deeper. He closed his eyes and tried to picture himself as a nine-year-old again. There he was, his brown hair poking out in all directions, looking up at the beams with a determined expression on his face. There was no darkness. There were no Patrol members who would fire crossbows at him if they heard the slightest splash. There was only the bridge and a game to be played.

"No fear," Jesse whispered, refusing to look at the swirling waters. That was what he and Eli always said when they played their games.

With that, he jumped up and grabbed the first beam

with both hands, nearly slamming his head against the underside of the bridge in the process. *I guess I don't have to jump as high as I did when I was nine.*

Jesse stretched out his hand to the second beam, swinging silently to it. That was another advantage the years had given him. When he was younger, he had to swing back and forth to get enough momentum, then launch into the air, hoping that he would be able to reach the next beam. If he did not, Eli, the Sea Serpent, would be waiting to get him in the river below. Jesse could almost picture him now, green scum coating his black hair as he laughed and splashed, trying to get Jesse to fall.

But I will not fall. Another rung. This time, Jesse had to pause for a moment before moving on. His arms held his full weight, dangling him inches from the water. *I can't rest,* he thought desperately. *I can't hold on long enough for that.*

Hand over hand, beam over beam. Each time, Jesse's hand got farther away from the next beam. On the eighth, he had to use what little energy he had to swing back and gain momentum. Somewhere in the back of his memory, he knew there were twelve beams.

He lunged forward again, giving a short gasp. *Surely the sound of the river will cover the noise.* Evidently none of the Patrol had heard his heavy breathing, because no one came to investigate.

Jesse kept going, ignoring the pain. Clinging to the eleventh beam, he reached out his hand and grabbed nothing but air. For a second, he felt his lungs tighten in panic. *Trapped!* Then he looked closer. *No, it's still there. I just didn't reach far enough.*

Come on, just like with Eli.

The exhausted part of Jesse's mind mocked this idea. *No more games! It was never this hard in those days. You know you can't reach it.*

No! With every bit of energy his tired arms could force, Jesse swung back and let go with both hands, trusting they would find the twelfth beam.

They did, barely. Jesse had to claw the beam before he had enough of a grip to hold his weight. Then, with one last jump, Jesse collapsed on the bank.

Panting, he poked his head from beneath the bridge. The Patrol members were still by the bonfire. One of them was singing some loud, senseless tune that made the others roar with laughter.

Jesse limped into the forest, still glancing over his shoulder to make sure none of them would see him and begin pursuit. Only among the trees did he finally kneel to rest. He had made it. Eli would be proud of him.

Yes, I made it, but can I make it back?

Jesse shook his head and limped into the trees. His father always told him never to worry about something until worrying would do any good.

Kayne had trained him well. It didn't take Jesse long to identify the knob willow tree. He peeled the bark off in strips. Not knowing how much would be enough, he took an armful, just to be safe.

And how will I carry it across the river? Jesse knew he couldn't swing from support to support with only one arm. He quickly took off his belt, looping it around the stack and cinching it tight. It would not do to have the bark slip and fall into the river. *I can hold the strap between my teeth.*

No you can't, the practical side of him realized. *You won't even be able to cross under the bridge again. You're too tired!*

Lacking any other ideas, Jesse ignored his thoughts. He walked back to the bridge beside the road. Behind him, he could feel the shadow of the Suspicion Mountains looming into the dark. Everything was silent and calm, except for the rushing of the river. *A nice change from the inn today.*

Without knowing why, Jesse looked up. There, in the clear night sky, were thousands of stars, pricks of silver light against the blackness. "It's beautiful," he whispered.

He remembered stories his father had told him about the pictures that the stars formed, the heroes and villains of old whose mighty deeds were captured forever in the skies. Ever since his parents' disappearance, Jesse had not even stepped out of the inn after curfew. Uncle Tristan strictly forbade it, worried that a Patrol member might see Jesse and close down his inn. It had been a long time since Jesse had seen the stars the stories were based on.

Somehow, the starry sky made Jesse feel a little more confident. *This is my chance to do something heroic.*

Those warm feelings disappeared instantly as he reached the edge of the forest by the river. There were no Patrol members around the bonfire on the other side.

Where are they, then? Jesse ducked behind the nearest tree and peered out at the river. There they were, sitting beside the bank. One had his boots off and his legs in the water.

Clearly, he could not go back the same way he came. Jesse gripped the bundle of bark tighter. *I'll have to cross on the bridge.*

Of course, the short distance between the trees and the bridge would be the most dangerous, since there was no place for him to hide if one of the Patrol members looked his way. After that, he could crawl across the bridge, using its stone sides to shield him from detection.

But it would hurt, Jesse knew, putting full weight on his mangled leg as he crawled. *There is no other way,* he thought, gritting his teeth. *I have to do it.*

With that parting thought, he crouched down on the ground and crawled toward the bridge, pausing only when he reached the cold stone.

"What was that?" one Patrol member asked sharply. Jesse froze, his heart beating so fast he was sure they would hear it and discover the source of the sound.

"You're imagining things," another said.

Jesse eased his gaze over the stone wall of the bridge, hoping the darkness would hide him from sight. The largest Patrol member had stood, and was scanning the surrounding area for any further sign of movement.

"No," he said slowly. "I saw someone move."

"Could've been a bird."

"A bird the size of a human?"

Jesse's heart started to beat faster. "No," the Patrol member said. "Someone's there. I know it. And I've never been wrong."

Just when Jesse was considering diving over the stone wall of the bridge and into the river, an arrow cut through the air with a sharp sigh, landing among the Patrol members. They looked frantically around for the source of the threat, crossbows at the ready.

One bent down to pick up the arrow, eyes still fixed on the darkness. "This isn't a crude homemade arrow," he said, a tinge of fear in his voice.

Peasants, of course, were not permitted to own weapons. Swords, spears, and bows were reserved for the king, his guards and nobility, and Patrol members. It was the law. Still, Jesse knew that many created their own weapons for protection, or, in the case of the Rebellion, to fight against the king.

The Patrol member fingered the feathers that formed the shaft. "Blood red," he said ominously.

"A saard," his comrade breathed, glancing all around at the woods and stepping closer to the others.

Saards, according to legend in Mir, were the souls of those who had been killed on false charges. Denied justice in life, they sought it in death, punishing those who were responsible for their death. Red was their color, the color of bloodshed.

The fact that the Patrol member was afraid of the saard said much about his integrity. Jesse wondered how many bribes he had taken, how many innocent people he had knowingly condemned. It happened often, he knew, but the thought still made him sick.

But Father said there's no such being as a saard, Jesse remembered. *Who shot that arrow, then?*

There. By the mill. Beside the great wooden wheel that moved slowly with the river were two shadowy forms.

Silas and Rae. It has to be. They followed me here.

Jesse knew it wouldn't take long for the Patrol members to notice the same thing he had. He also knew that Silas would not kill any of the Patrol. The Youth Guard was sworn to protect the kingdom, not destroy its guards. *I have to do something before they are discovered.* Jesse knew that his size would hardly intimidate them. But if they believed he was a saard....

Without giving himself time to think about it further, Jesse set down the willow bark on the bridge. Hands shaking with fear, he stood and faced the Patrol members, staring down at them from his position on the bridge.

The one who had been so afraid of the saard arrow pointed at him, staggering backwards. "There he is," Jesse heard him whisper. *A strong, grown man afraid of a boy. Surely the man has something on his conscience.*

"What business do you have?" another questioned, his hand on his crossbow. Even he seemed to have lost the customary bluster of a Patrol member. Jesse thought for a second about how he must look to them. Pale, homemade clothing, loose on his small frame, blowing in the wind. Light brown hair, almost gray in the moonlight. *Just like a saard.*

"I have come to find the ones who killed my parents," he said calmly, his mind struggling to come up with a satisfactory story. He spoke clearly, but quietly, not a trace of the fear he felt showing in his voice. "After their passing, with no one to provide for me, I starved to death. It was not right."

"Many go without food in these hard times," one shot back. "It was not our fault."

"Wasn't it?" Jesse never looked away from them. "You are the Patrol. It is your job to protect, in the name of the king."

"Begone, foul creature," one Patrol member said, raising his crossbow.

Jesse tried to duck to the ground, but found that his feet would not obey his mind's command. He was frozen to the bridge, unable to move.

"No!" the other said quickly, shoving his friend's arm down. "Would you add to our guilt? Besides, you know the saards cannot be killed."

"It was you who shot the arrow?" the man with the crossbow said suspiciously. Jesse nodded. "Prove it."

For a second, Jesse panicked. Then the solution came to him. Without daring a glance at the mill, he spoke confidently and loudly, "All I have to do is raise my arm, like this."

Sure enough, a split second later, a second arrow pierced the ground near the Patrol member's foot. All three men stared in the direction of the mill.

"My father," Jesse said simply. "He does not wish to be seen, because of his disfigurement. My mother is there too. Both were killed by Patrol members."

For all Jesse knew, the story could be true. The thought brought him a sharp twinge of pain, and he pushed it away.

He pointed at the Patrol member in the middle, the one who had been so afraid of the saard arrow and had tried to shoot him with his crossbow. "Was it you, sir?"

He did not answer, and Jesse wondered if perhaps this man did have blood on his hands. "I could raise my arm again,"

Jesse said. The man's face froze. "My father would not miss this time."

A pause. "But I choose not to," Jesse finished, stepping back. Then, slowly, with effort, he climbed up on the stone wall of the bridge. A misstep would land him in the river, and he commanded his legs not to shake with fear.

"I choose instead to show mercy." Then, quieter, "Mercy that was not shown to me or my family."

The Patrol members looked up at him in terror. "Begone from here!" Jesse commanded. With that ringing shout, Jesse jumped off the bridge.

For a moment, falling through the air, he thought he was wrong, that his memory had failed him after all these years. But then, there it was, cold and sharp: the jutting stone that he and Eli had often used to climb onto the bridge from the river. He held onto the stone with all of his strength.

Jesse had only tried this trick once, six years before, trying to impress Eli, no doubt. He had leapt off the bridge, reaching out to catch the stone sticking out from the side so that he would jerk to a stop before hitting the water. He had missed, and Eli had laughed at him when he emerged, sputtering, from the river.

This time, though, I did not miss. Jesse hung there for a few seconds, gripping the stone until his arms ached. Anyone on the far side of the bridge would see a foolish boy dangling from a ledge of the bridge. But to the guards on the other side, the pale saard boy had disappeared into thin air.

Sure enough, he heard a shout of dismay, then running footsteps. Jesse clung to the rock for as long as he could, with every muscle in his body crying out in protest. Then he let go and fell into the river.

As soon as he hit the cold water, he clawed frantically at the bank so the current wouldn't drag him away. He tried to pull himself up, but the force of the river was too strong and his arms too weak. Panic swirled inside of him, faster and more furious than the river. *I'm going to drown!*

Two brown boots flashed in front of Jesse's eyes. "Take my hand," a low voice said. Jesse reached up, gasping as he let go of the bank and felt the river begin to pull him away. Then he felt a large, warm hand clasp his, and his body was lifted into the air.

Jesse sputtered, coughing up the water he had swallowed, and crawled to his knees. Silas looked down on him, and Rae stood off to the side, watching them.

"Take the bark to Kayne," Jesse said to her, pointing weakly to the bridge where he had left the bundle.

Rae nodded. Jesse wasn't sure, since it was dark, but he thought he might have seen a glimmer of approval on her face. With a graceful leap, she jumped over the bridge's high stone wall and carried the bark through the sleeping streets of Mir, moving like a silent wisp of wind.

"You did well," Silas said, nodding at him. He handed Jesse his cloak, then turned toward the road, gesturing for him to follow.

And even though Jesse was wet, sore, and shaking with cold and fear, he smiled as he looked up at the heroes in the stars.

CHAPTER 5

The first thing Kayne did when Jesse entered the shack was give him a sharp rap on the forehead.

"What was that for?" Jesse demanded, jerking back and rubbing the sore area.

"Making sure your skull isn't hollow," Kayne grumbled, stooping back down to the rug where Parvel was lying. "Seems it ain't, which means you're not brainless. Just stupid."

Jesse just grinned. The smile faded from his face as he glanced down at Parvel, whose eyes twitched slightly under his lids. "Are you going to give him the antidote?"

"Already did," Kayne said. "I had the water boiling and ready."

Jesse smiled to himself. That meant, no matter what Kayne said, he had believed Jesse would come back with the knob willow bark.

"It's not working," Rae pronounced, staring at Parvel's still form.

"Not yet," Silas countered. Jesse had soon realized that in addition to being a near-perfect aim with a longbow, Silas

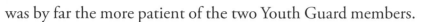

was by far the more patient of the two Youth Guard members.

Rae just grunted and went back to pacing, covering the same ground she had ever since they entered Kayne's shack.

"It'll work," Kayne promised, nodding in satisfaction. "Faster than a lot of…. Confound it, girl, will you stop that pacing? This isn't military school, you know."

To Jesse's surprise, Rae actually stopped, choosing instead to tap her foot against the table leg as she waited.

Looking at Parvel's flushed, pained face, Jesse almost wished that he could pray to Parvel's God. *But even if He does exist,* he thought bitterly, *He certainly isn't taking care of His own very well.*

Jesse turned to Silas and asked a question that had been on his mind since the bridge. "Why did you have arrows with red shafts? In Mir, that's the mark of a saard. It's their color."

"Parvel's idea," Silas said shortly. "We dyed them before leaving the capital. He's from this district and is familiar with local legend."

"Care to tell me how that knowledge was useful?"

Everyone jerked their heads down at the sound of Parvel's weak voice. He opened his eyes, wincing as if even that small movement was painful, and blinked at the people staring at him.

"We'll explain later," Jesse said. "Can we get you anything?"

Parvel blinked at him. "Who are you? What's your name?"

"Jesse."

Parvel stared at him thoughtfully. "What's wrong?" Jesse asked.

"Nothing," Parvel said. "It's just that…you remind me of someone I once knew. The same green eyes…." Then he shook his head, wincing at the pain it caused him. "May I have some water?"

Jesse dipped a metal cup into the bucket from the well and handed it to Parvel. He fumbled with it, spilling most of it on his sweat-soaked shirt, and downed the rest in one gulp. "Thank you. Now, tell me, what happened?"

He doesn't know, Jesse realized. *All he knows is that he woke up here, lying on the ground, with a paste smeared on his arm.*

Kayne explained about the poisoned arrow and how Jesse had gotten the antidote. Jesse couldn't help but feel a little proud at that part of the story.

"Thank you," Parvel said simply, nodding at him. "You probably saved my life."

Jesse coughed and looked down. "It was just lucky Rae and Silas came to the inn."

"I'm sure luck had nothing to do with it," Parvel said, a small smile appearing on his face. Jesse remembered what Rae had said about Parvel believing in God.

I don't want to hear about it. The village priest said it was God's will that his parents left. *If that's how God treats us, then I have no use for Him.*

"This poison," Jesse said, turning to Kayne. "How long before it wears off? When will he recover?"

Kayne shook his head. "No bothering about that, now. This boy needs his rest." He started to pull Silas and Rae away from the sickbed.

Silas didn't move. "We need to know."

Something in his flat tone must have convinced Kayne. "This kind of poison is strange, that's for sure," Kayne said, refusing to look at Silas. "Antidote counters the poison, but it doesn't get rid of it. Not all the way. Besides, I've never seen a case this bad. There'll be more spells of fever as his body tries to get rid of the poison."

"For how long?" Parvel asked.

"Best guess? A few weeks."

Weeks?

Jesse was sure his expression mirrored the shock on Parvel's face. "Very well, then," he said heavily. "I would like to speak with Rae and Silas alone, if it's not too much trouble."

"'Course," Kayne said, standing with effort, his old bones creaking. "Always love bein' thrown out of my own home by complete strangers."

"I'll make more of the dispur poultice," Jesse said, hurrying out to the kitchen. He reached for the cabinet, then paused. *I wonder what they're talking about.* He could hear the rumble of low voices in the other room.

Maybe it wouldn't hurt to listen to a little. He edged the curtain open a crack and peered in. Silas and Rae leaned over Parvel as he eased himself up, leaning heavily on his good arm.

"You cannot go on with two members," Parvel reasoned. "Squads are supposed to have four."

"We'll wait for you," Silas insisted.

"No," Parvel said firmly.

Silas was not about to give up. "Parvel, you are our squad captain. We will not leave you behind."

"And I'm telling you that someone knows we are here, and they clearly want us dead."

Jesse shivered at the calm way in which he spoke. "Once the man with the crossbow realizes you are alive, he will be back," Parvel continued.

"He won't be back. Ever," Silas countered simply. "I shot him."

Parvel thought about this for a moment. "Members of the Rebellion never work alone. There could be others, and they have ways of finding those they want to kill. I will not see our mission fail before it has begun."

There was silence for a moment. "He's right," Rae said at last. "We need to get away from here." She stood and began to pace again, as if preparing for an attack. "As soon as possible."

"Listen to me." Parvel leaned toward them. "I will not have you playing games with death. There is a good chance you will die on this mission. That is why I refuse to rush into danger without thinking about what happens after. And neither should you."

"Here he goes again," Rae muttered.

"I don't think this is a game, if that's what you mean," Silas said, his voice flat. "I know the danger."

"You play the game simply by being alive, Silas. After all, we all die, some sooner than others. Without God, what happens after death? Are you content to step into a black void of nothingness, to fade out of existence?"

"Give it a rest, Parvel," was all Rae said, waving him off. "You won't convert me, not with all your sermons. You should have become a priest instead of joining the Guard."

Interesting. Jesse had always been taught that religion was for the weak, the old, and children who did not know any better. *Yet, here is a Youth Guard member, the strongest and bravest in the land, who believes in God.*

"You must leave," Parvel said, "but not alone." His next words froze Jesse to the floor. "Take Jesse."

CHAPTER 6

Jesse decided his hearing must have failed him, or that he had gone crazy, or that he was back at the inn, dreaming in his bed. Those were the only reasonable explanations for Parvel's words.

"Parvel, are you thinking clearly?" Silas asked in disbelief. "He was not trained for this like we were."

Rae was not quite so kind. "He's small, weak, and crippled," she pointed out. "He would die before we even began the mission. Your mind must have been affected by this fever of yours, Parvel."

She's right, Jesse knew, his heart sinking. *They're both right.* Anyone could see why he was not fit for the Guard.

So he was surprised when Parvel spoke up again. "Physical strength alone does not qualify a person to join the Youth Guard," Parvel said. "There are other traits that are much more important—courage, determination, intelligence. He has those traits."

Rae just snorted, but Silas nodded thoughtfully. "That may be so," he said. "But the fact remains: he is not of the Guard."

"Perhaps he should have been."

"But he is not," Rae said forcefully. "And we are sworn never to reveal our mission. Only the king and the captain of the Patrol know of it."

"As captain of this squad, I have the right to make any decision I wish, if I believe it is for the good of the group."

"Oh," Rae said bitterly, "so now you are going to assert your authority over us."

"No." Parvel sighed heavily. "I will not. We will vote."

Jesse, still listening, did not know what to do. On one hand, everything in him leaped at the chance to join the Guard. It was all he had ever dreamed of. *But what if I slow them down or keep them from accomplishing their mission?*

"Silas and I can do it on our own," Rae insisted.

"There are some things you cannot do on your own," Parvel said forcefully.

Jesse wondered if that was really true. Rae and Silas had proven to be among the most able young people in the kingdom. They certainly did not need him.

"This is what we trained for," Rae continued. "It will be a loss not to have you with us, of course, but we'll come back for you after we have successfully completed the mission."

"Rae," Parvel said solemnly, "there is a reason that four is the minimum for squads. Even three is inadequate for the danger you will face. You would be knowingly sabotaging your chances of success by continuing with any less. You do not understand the danger of these missions."

"And you do?" Rae said it like a challenge, her arms crossed in defiance.

"Yes," Parvel said, but it was more like an anguished cry than an answer. He slumped back down on the straw, like he had used all of his strength in that one word. "Yes, I do."

There was silence for a moment. Rae clearly had no further objections.

"The vote, then," Silas said. "We know where you stand, Parvel." He sighed. "And, although it goes against all of the common sense I have, I will stand with my captain. Jesse will come with us."

Frozen to the ground, Jesse stared disbelievingly at him through a crack in the curtain. He had not expected the tall, stoic archer to side with him. *No*, he corrected himself. *He is siding with Parvel, out of a sense of duty. He doesn't really believe that I can do it.*

"I disagree, of course," Rae said, her arms crossed in defiance, "but I suppose that doesn't matter at all."

"Very good," Parvel said. "I can do little now except pray for your safety."

Rae snorted. "Don't waste your energy," she said. "I decided long ago that either God doesn't exist, or He's deaf to the cries of good, hurting people."

"You are wrong about that, Rae," Parvel said quietly, "for it was when I was hurting the most that I cried out to God, and He answered me. Sometimes you have to come to the end of your own strength to hear God. You have to stop fighting."

Jesse could see Rae stiffen. "I will never stop fighting. Never."

"Then perhaps that is why you've never heard Him." There was silence for a moment. Rae clearly had no more to say.

Then Parvel rolled on his side, turning toward the kitchen. "You may come out, Jesse."

Jesse felt his face flush, and was grateful that no one could see in the dark as he stepped into the room. *Parvel knew that I was listening.*

"This is very serious business, Jesse," Parvel said, shifting to look at him. Jesse noticed that his words were beginning to slur together slightly. "It is great honor, but you must remember that few of the Youth Guard ever return."

"Many of them die far from home, are slain in battle by the enemy, or become lost, stranded, or held captive in a foreign land," Rae said, her voice betraying no emotion. "You will face death by starvation, assassins, drowning, bandits, and countless other dangers."

"And you have not received the proper training," Silas added.

"Chances are high that you won't survive," Rae said, stepping toward him. Jesse thought she was smiling, mocking him. "It would be no shame for you to refuse."

I bet you want me to. Jesse's head told him that Silas and Rae were right. He could die on the mission. He was not ready for that kind of danger. He should not go with them.

But something else, something deep inside him, disagreed. *What's the good of living like this? Staying with my aunt and uncle, doing the same chores every day, while people mock me behind my back for my crippled leg? This could be my only chance to prove myself.*

"No," Jesse said, shaking his head. "I will go with you."

"Shouldn't you ask your mother and father?" Jesse gritted his teeth at the scorn in Rae's voice.

"My mother and father are dead," he said. That was the easiest explanation. They didn't need to know about the disappearance. They would ask too many questions—questions Jesse couldn't answer. "I live with my aunt and uncle. I don't think they'll miss me if I go."

"Except that your pig of an uncle will have to throw his table scraps to his dog instead of you," Kayne grumbled from the darkness, barging back into the house.

"Kayne," Jesse scolded, his face turning red, "don't say that. They take care of me." He couldn't believe he was defending his aunt and uncle, but he didn't want anyone's pity.

"Funny story I'll have to tell tomorrow when Tristan and Dara come knocking on my door," Kayne said. "I was all asleep in my bed when I heard a ruckus outside. Patrol member had ahold of young Jesse, hollerin' about him breakin' curfew. Poor boy got hauled off before I could say a word. Who knows where they'll take him? The prison in the capital maybe, or one of the king's work gangs."

Jesse slowly started to smile. "It might work."

"Your friend can stay here, I suppose," Kayne continued, "provided he doesn't do any gripin' and makes himself useful when he's strong enough. I don't approve of charity."

"I will do anything I am able to do," Parvel promised.

Silas walked over to Jesse and placed a hand on his shoulder. "You risked your life to save Parvel," he said quietly. "For that, I am willing to give you a chance. We leave as soon as the sun comes up." He walked outside, to collect supplies,

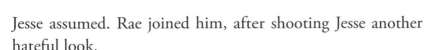

Jesse assumed. Rae joined him, after shooting Jesse another hateful look.

Head spinning, Jesse sat down on the floor beside Parvel. *Me, a Youth Guard member.*

Parvel grinned weakly and licked his dry lips. "Well, it appears we have a fourth squad member after all."

One thought echoed over and over in Jesse's mind: *Do I really want to do this?* He wasn't entirely sure. *But it's too late. I can't turn back now.*

"I hope you were listening to what I said to Rae," Parvel continued. "It was important."

With great effort, Jesse held back a groan. *Rae was right. Parvel should have become a priest.* "Why would you say that?"

"Remember when I said you reminded me of someone?" Jesse nodded. Parvel stared straight at him. "That person was my brother."

Jesse knew that the pain on Parvel's face was from more than the poison. *I wonder what happened to him?* He was too afraid to actually ask Parvel the question.

"Listen to me, Jesse," Parvel said, and though his voice was weak, his words were not. "My brother lived his life denying God, believing that he was good enough, strong enough and clever enough to save himself. Do not make the same mistake he did."

"My father always said that we don't need God around here. We take care of ourselves."

"That's what my brother said too," Parvel said, turning away. "I wonder if I should even have asked you to join the squad. Now, more than ever, you are playing with death."

"Parvel…." Jesse sighed, and his words came out in a tangled jumble. "Silas and Rae had to come and rescue me tonight. I don't think they even want me. No one has ever expected anything out of me beyond feeding the chickens and washing tables. If I had gone to the muster, no one would have given me a second look. Besides…."

"Promise me, Jesse," Parvel said. His hazel eyes were glassy. *The fever is returning.* Jesse took the cloth from his forehead and dipped it in new water. "Promise."

Jesse replaced the cloth. "Promise what?"

"Never leave them," Parvel said quietly, as if he didn't want anyone to hear. "My brother only cared about himself. Justice. Maybe that's what happened to him."

He's not making any sense, Jesse thought. "You need to rest, Parvel."

"I wanted to go too, but you wouldn't let me," he muttered, forcing his eyes open a slit. "Justice…promise me."

He's fading fast, Jesse knew. He only hoped Kayne was right and that it was just another spell of weakness. But it could not be denied that with his pale face and shaking body, Parvel looked like he was dying.

"I promise," Jesse said. But Parvel had already closed his eyes. Jesse jerked forward in alarm, then sat back. Parvel was still breathing.

Justice. Why is Parvel obsessed with justice? Maybe it was nothing but the fever, making Parvel's words slip into nonsense, but regardless, Jesse had made a promise never to leave Rae and Silas behind. *I'm more worried they'll leave me.*

The next hour was a flurry of activity. Silas hurried back to the inn to get the horses from Uncle Tristan's stables, tethering them to a tree outside of Kayne's shack. Jesse had no possessions to bring except a few supplies Kayne loaned him, so he was put in charge of attending to Parvel. Rae simply stood, glaring at Jesse at every opportunity. Kayne blustered around and tied more supplies into a tight bundle, including some of the black willow bark. "Just in case," he said.

Every quarter of an hour, Jesse changed the cloth on Parvel's forehead, as he murmured more strings of nonsense. Kayne had promised to keep him out of sight, but Jesse wondered how he could hide a raving invalid for a full month. When one citizen of Mir learned a piece of news, so did the whole village.

"We'll be back, Parvel," Jesse said quietly, standing from his post. "All of us."

He could only hope he was speaking the truth.

Kayne hobbled over to Jesse, staring up at him, his gnarled face twisted into a serious expression. "You sure about this, boy? You really want to risk your life following two strangers into danger and near certain death?"

Kayne has an interesting way of putting things. Jesse sighed. "I know it doesn't make sense, but…." His voice trailed off as he tried to explain his thoughts. "I have to do this. I've always dreamed of adventure, and I can't stay here in Mir all my life. I need something more."

Kayne just grunted. "Knew you'd say that. The trouble with you, boy—well, there's a lot of troubles with you, but one of 'em is that you think with your heart instead of your head. It'll get you nothin' but a heap of trouble."

"Maybe," Jesse shot back, "but if I had thought with my head instead of my heart tonight, Parvel might be dead."

Slowly, Kayne began to nod. "True enough. True enough. Well, you're fifteen. Plenty old enough to make your own choices." He shook a finger at Jesse. "I ought to stop you. Take you back to your aunt and uncle. That'd be the responsible thing."

"I don't think you *could* stop me."

"Knew you'd say that too." Kayne grinned briefly, and Jesse caught a glimpse of two rows of crooked teeth. "Stubborn as a knotty pine branch. I like that about you." He jerked his head toward his bedroom. "Come with me."

Jesse followed him, ducking through a low doorway. Kayne reached under his low bed. "I want you to have this," he said gruffly. He handed Jesse an elaborately carved walking stick.

Jesse's eyes widened as he stared at the upraised leaves and animals. In the dim light of the candle, he could see, though the designs were simple, each was unique and unmistakable.

"It's not quite done," Kayne added, almost apologetically, eyes glancing down to a blank portion near the bottom. "I was goin' to give it to you on your sixteenth birthday this winter."

"I've never seen anything like it," Jesse breathed. He set it on the ground and gripped it. *A perfect fit.*

"You'll need it on your journey. It's good, strong wood," Kayne said, nodding at it. Then he looked up at Jesse. "And, come flood or famine, battle or brawl, whatever hardships it goes through, it won't break. You can count on that."

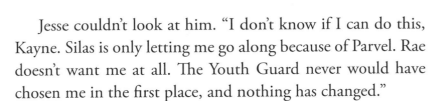

Jesse couldn't look at him. "I don't know if I can do this, Kayne. Silas is only letting me go along because of Parvel. Rae doesn't want me at all. The Youth Guard never would have chosen me in the first place, and nothing has changed."

Kayne just stood silently for a moment. Then he spoke. "Look at the staff. Every symbol has a purpose." He pointed to the animals carved at different heights in the wood. "A river tortoise, always determined. The phoenix, the wisest of all the birds. A mink, fiercely loyal to its kind."

Jesse ran his hand over the designs, but didn't say anything.

"I chose those designs on purpose, you know," Kayne said. "You think these old hands started making this staff a few moments ago, after those Guard members chose you?" He answered his own question. "No. I've been working on this for years, with you in mind."

Kayne turned to leave the room. "Now, if you're going to leave, you'd better get moving before your overbearing relatives break my door down lookin' for you."

With his left hand, Jesse gripped the walking stick and took a step. Kayne was right; it would bear the weight of his crippled leg and make travel on foot much easier.

"Come." Jesse looked up to see Silas standing in the doorway. "It is dawn."

CHAPTER 7

"Wasteland Road, Desolation Ravine, Way of Tears," Silas read from the signpost at the foot of the mountains. "Cheery names you people from District One have," he said dryly, looking at Jesse.

He shrugged, reigning in his horse—or rather, Kayne's horse—behind Silas. "Each one has a story. People in Mir, and the other villages near the mountains, love stories. It's part of who we are."

"A foolish waste of time," Rae said, with an air of arrogant confidence that made Jesse wish she was lying sick at Kayne's house instead of Parvel. Even her horse, a chestnut with a carefully groomed mane, held its head high.

Jesse's horse, on the other hand, was a ragged beast who snorted dirt out of his nose every once in a while. Jesse called him Fleas.

They had left Mir behind as quickly as possible, never traveling on the main road. Jesse was glad they had not encountered any Patrol. Curfew officially ended when the sun rose, but it had only barely peaked above the horizon when they left.

Even now, the orange dawn showed no other travelers on the road, although Jesse knew it would soon be crowded with Festival visitors anxious to return home.

Silas fumbled around in his pack with one hand, holding tightly onto the reigns with the other. It was clear that before his training at the capital, he'd had little experience with horses. He pulled out a folded parchment—a map of the kingdom—and studied it carefully.

"Which way?" Rae prompted, shifting in her saddle. She glanced from side to side constantly, and Jesse could tell that she didn't like being out in the open without any place to hide.

"Be patient," Silas said. Although he didn't raise his voice—he never seemed to raise it—Jesse could see a spark of irritation in his eyes. Especially on a horse, he towered over Jesse, and his lean frame showed plenty of muscle. He kept his quiver of arrows and longbow with him at all times, although Rae had pointed out that a sword was an easier weapon to take on a journey. *Level-headed and cautious*, Jesse decided.

Rae, on the other hand, seemed to have been chosen for her fiery personality and desire for action. Her black hair fell to her shoulders, and she wore a short tunic dress over leather trousers, a sword at her side. Jesse didn't doubt that she knew how to use it.

"We travel north," Silas said slowly.

Everything in Jesse wanted to ask where they were going, what their mission was, but he forced himself to stay quiet. *Rae, at least, would take the opportunity to make another harsh comment about the secrecy of the mission. Better to wait.*

"The Way of Tears leads to my own home in the east, District Two," Silas continued. "The most direct route north is the Wasteland Road…."

"If you wish to be robbed by bandits," Jesse interjected. "Believe me, that's not a wise choice."

Silas nodded. "Helpful advice," he said. "Then there is Desolation Ravine." He pointed straight ahead of them to the wide highway.

"That's what I would suggest," Jesse said. "The road is safe, fairly level, and well-traveled."

"Exactly why we must avoid it at all costs," Rae said. "No one must identify us as Guard members, especially now that we suspect someone wants to kill us."

Silas stared ahead at Desolation Ravine, and Jesse knew what he saw: a road scarred by the tracks and ditches formed by many years of wagons and carts cutting through. Today, of all days of the year, the road would be crowded with people. "Perhaps Rae is right," Silas said.

"But if we can't take any of the three roads, then what do we do?" Jesse asked in frustration. "*Fly* over the mountains?"

Rae looked at him in disgust. "Of course not." She pointed to a narrow gorge a few paces off. "We go that way."

Jesse shook his head. "That road is not marked for a reason. It's not a road at all, just a gorge where a stream cuts through the mountain. I've heard of it. It goes high up into the mountains on narrow trails. I doubt the horses can manage."

Rae crossed her arms and eyed him levelly. "They are strong horses, used to traveling. They can handle any terrain.

The question is, can you?"

Jesse tried to ignore the jab. He turned to Silas, knowing he was the only one worth persuading. "It's too dangerous. We don't know what the high road is like."

"It's better than finding ourselves dead on the side of the main highway by nightfall," Rae shot back. "We can't be seen."

Silas sighed and put the map back in his bag. "I must agree with Rae. We take the higher road."

Why don't they understand? I know this land. I know the dangers better than they do, even with all their training. Jesse gritted his teeth in frustration. Perhaps he should just go along with the others. But what if he was right? "Silas...."

But Silas had already kicked his horse, which jolted forward with a lurch. Jesse noticed that the horse needed some coaxing to keep from following the main path.

"Try to keep up," Rae said, smirking at him as she edged her horse in front of Jesse's. She guided her mount with pressure from her ankles, keeping her hands completely free. *So that she can use her sword,* Jesse knew. *Well, with what we may face on this road, we may need Rae's skill with a blade.*

"Come on, Fleas," Jesse muttered, following behind them. He was now the weakest member of the squad, and he knew it. Worse, Silas and Rae knew it. *I suppose I can expect more of the same until I prove myself.*

Jesse wondered if he would ever have the chance.

Slowly, the path began to slope upward, into the crags of the Suspicion Mountains. By the time the sun was high in the sky, Fleas was beginning to limp slightly. Jesse could feel it.

He was not bred to travel on jagged stone, Jesse knew. *None of them were.* Soon, all three horses would be worn out completely. *I have to say something.*

Jesse spurred Fleas on and stopped in front of Silas and Rae. "We must not continue on horseback," he said.

Silas scowled at him, gripping the reins tightly as his horse swayed from the sudden stop. "Are you mad?"

He doesn't know anything about horses, Jesse reminded himself, forcing himself to speak patiently. "The road will only get higher and harder. One misstep, and we'll tumble off the cliff. These horses aren't as sure-footed as the pack mules that normally travel the mountains. They will not survive the journey, and we may not either."

Rae laughed disdainfully. "Some risks are necessary on a mission like this. It would take many days to make this journey on foot."

That made Jesse's blood boil. Unlike Silas, she *did* know horses. She must know he spoke the truth, yet she refused to admit it. *And why? Because she stubbornly clings to her own plan, her own desire to lead.*

This time, though, Jesse did not back down. "Either we loose the horses and let them turn back," he said, "or we turn back ourselves."

"We will do nothing of the kind," Rae said. "We would lose a full day's travel. Giana and I are just fine with this road."

Rae nudged her horse forward toward him, and Fleas took a nervous step backward, coming uncomfortably close to the edge of the cliff. "Afraid of heights, are you, Jesse?"

Jesse refused to look down, refused to judge the distance between the road and the stream below. It was not far yet, he knew, but it would be a nasty fall just the same. Giana, responding to Rae's command, whinnied as she took another step forward.

"Enough," Silas commanded.

Rae pulled back. "Who made you captain?" she said spitefully.

"I am not the one acting like a child here," Silas said. Rae glowered at him, and for a moment, Jesse was happy that her rage was directed at someone other than himself. "We will go forward," Silas said, "but carefully." He did not look back at Jesse.

Fine. If that's how they want it. "On to our death," he muttered. "All hail the Youth Guard."

Nearly an hour later, the trail narrowed further. Silas' entire body was stiff, and Jesse knew that he felt the fear of any inexperienced horseman on dangerous terrain. In contrast, Rae was as relaxed as if they were strolling through an open meadow.

"We should be halfway through the mountains by now," she called back. "It will be a downhill climb from now on."

While Rae looked back, Giana, the regal chestnut she rode, took a hesitant step forward. Jesse watched in horror as the loose stones fell away beneath her back hooves.

"Look out!"

It was too late. Rae's sharp cry pierced the gorge as Giana lost her footing and began to tip over the edge. Rae pushed off from Giana and grabbed onto the ledge.

Jesse was off his horse in a second, and Silas, dismounting rather awkwardly, was not far behind him.

But Rae did not need their help. After a quick scramble to get her footing on the cliff wall, she pulled herself up with little more than a grunt. She crawled back onto the path and stood, dusting herself off. If Jesse had not seen a glimpse of her wide, dark eyes, he would not have guessed that she was the least bit shaken.

Giana did not fare as well. She lay at the bottom of the gorge, near the stream, crying out in pain the way only a wounded horse can.

Silas glanced at Jesse. He just shook his head. *There is no way any horse could survive that fall.* Silas nodded and stepped forward, reaching for an arrow from his quiver.

"No," Rae said, her face set in determination. "You might miss. I don't want her to be in anymore pain. I'll do it."

Carefully, Rae climbed down the gorge, keeping a sure footing on outcroppings and ramps formed by landslides. She pulled out her sword.

Jesse could not watch, and turned away. There was no place for him to go. He merely clutched Fleas' bridle until the deed was done, a sick feeling in his stomach.

Rae returned with their supplies on her back. Her sword was wiped clean, and her face was tight with anger. *Anger at whom? The horse? Silas? Me? She is the one who could have prevented this.*

"I suppose now we'll continue on foot," Jesse said.

Something in Rae's face snapped, and Jesse backed against the stone wall of the gorge to get away from her. She looked almost like she would punch him. Then she curled her hand into a tight fist and stormed away.

"This is not the time to congratulate yourself," Silas scolded him. "Can't you see that?"

Instantly, Jesse felt ashamed. Rae knew she was responsible for Giana's death. Maybe the person she was angry at was herself. *And I only made it worse.*

Jesse lifted the water skin, filled with water from the Dell River, and bag of supplies from Fleas. "You were a good horse after all," he told him, stroking his jagged mane. Fleas snorted in agreement.

Jesse slapped his flanks. "Go on," he called. "Follow the stream back to the river."

Of course, Fleas could hardly understand him, but he knew which way was downhill. Freed of his burdens, he loped away. *He will get to Mir by morning.*

Silas did the same to his horse. "We'd better catch up with Rae," he said. "Who knows how far along she is by now."

Jesse nodded and gripped his walking stick. It was now time to test Kayne's handiwork. They had a long way to go before dark, and he doubted either Silas or Rae would want to wait for him.

This is not how I expected the mission to begin. Suddenly, a hundred pictures flashed in his mind; Aunt Dara baking bread for the inn patrons, he and Eli pulling a prank on the pompous village priest, Kayne playing checkers with him, the butcher calling out for customers, the beggar on the corner who always called Jesse "son." Each one of them would be going to bed tonight safe and secure. It was all Jesse could do not to run after Fleas and go back home.

You're not one of them anymore, he reminded himself. *You are one of the Guard.* He remembered all the tales he had heard of the adventures of the Youth Guard. They were all so brave, so strong. He was not.

"Jesse!" Silas' voice cut into his thoughts. "Come on!"

Sighing, Jesse followed after him, planting his staff in front of him with each step. He had made a promise. Somehow, he would have to keep going.

CHAPTER 8

Hours later, each member of the group had fallen into a predictable role. Silas led the way, keeping a steady pace and occasionally checking the map for landmarks. Behind him, Rae followed in silence, which she broke only to ask how far they had traveled or to complain about the constant tapping of Jesse's staff against the rock. Jesse just plodded on, trying to ignore his aching body.

Silas' voice interrupted his thoughts. "It's getting late," he observed, stopping to take a drink out of his water skin.

Jesse looked up at the sinking sun. He had been awake since before dawn, but he had been afraid to slow down, since Rae and Silas showed no signs of tiring. "At least now that the trail is sloping downward, the travel is easier."

"True," Silas agreed. "A good day's journey. Wouldn't you agree, Rae?"

Rae just grunted and scrambled up the wall of the gorge, finding small crags and footholds Jesse would never have known existed.

Jesse and Silas didn't bother asking where she was going. From time to time, Rae would scale the wall of the gorge and look over into the nearby Desolation Ravine.

"I can't see what value it has," Silas said, "but it keeps her occupied."

"And the more time she spends scouting out the territory, the less time she has to be angry with us," Jesse finished.

For the first time that Jesse could remember, Silas smiled. "Exactly." They walked on in silence.

With a swirl of dust, Rae jumped down from a nearby boulder. Jesse jerked slightly, still not used to how she could sneak up on them without being seen or heard. "I saw some travelers by a signpost," she said. "We have a few more hours before we reach the end of the mountains."

"Good," Silas said, stopping on the trail. "We will stop here for the night, then." They had reached a place where the trail widened briefly, giving them enough room to comfortably set up camp. "It will be dark soon."

Darkness would not fall for nearly an hour, Jesse knew. He wondered if Silas was stopping early for his benefit, noticing his lagging pace as the day wore on.

He expected Rae to protest that they should continue on as long as there was light to see by. She just nodded. "I'll find some firewood." She had hardly said a word since they had abandoned the horses at noon.

It had been a long day. While he walked, Jesse had imagined himself slaying dragons, daringly attacking a foreign citadel, smuggling secret messages to the troops on the Northern Waste, and defeating powerful sorcerers. It was something to pass the time, and, besides, it was a way to keep his mind off his aching body.

His left arm, not used to the work of supporting his weight for so long, ached with every movement of the staff. He tried not to wince as he sat down on the rocky ground.

Rae was gone a long time, and Jesse felt uncomfortable in the silence. "Where are you from?" he asked Silas finally.

"Davior," he said, "a major city in District Two, near the Deep Mines. My mother is a weaver there."

"And your father?" Jesse asked politely.

"A priest."

"Oh." Jesse stared past him at the mountain. "So you're with Parvel, then? A believer in God?"

"My father died," Silas said shortly. "Any belief I had in God died with him."

Instantly, Jesse felt sympathy for Silas. *In some way, at least, I know what that feels like.* "I'm sorry."

"It was a long time ago." Silas leaned against the gorge wall. "So, I suppose you know why these are called the Suspicion Mountains."

Jesse nodded. "Before the king conquered what is now District Four, the mountains were the only thing that separated us from the hostile desert tribes."

"I thought District Four was a part of Amarias since the beginning."

Jesse shrugged. "Most people don't know much history, other than what happened in their own district a generation or so back. Travelers from all over the kingdom come to the inn, and I hear their stories."

"What do you know about the Abaktan Desert?"

It was Rae, who had somehow managed to climb up the cliff without making a sound. She unceremoniously dropped a few dry sticks and twigs on the path. "It's not much, but there aren't many trees in these mountains."

Silas rummaged around in his pack and pulled out the flint stone. Rae didn't seem concerned with the fire. She fixed her eyes on Jesse. "The Abaktan Desert," she repeated. "Have you heard about it?"

"So that's where we're going," Jesse said thoughtfully. That was not good news, but at least he knew. Then a thought occurred to him. He laughed. "And you expected to ride into the desert on horses?"

Rae glared at him. "During training, they didn't waste time with information about geography. Most of the time was spent on skills like sword fighting."

Incredulous, Jesse shook his head. "Don't they know that for any mission, knowledge is the most important weapon?"

Now it became clear why so many Youth Guard members died on their missions. Inexperienced young people blundered into unknown parts of the kingdom, facing countless dangers along the way.

"I agree," Silas said. He had managed to create a meager fire, just enough to keep them warm as the sun began to sink in the sky. "I myself wondered why we weren't told more."

"If we survive," Jesse said firmly, "I will make sure that King Selen adjusts this training period. It's foolish to plan missions like this, without proper training."

"I, for one, plan to survive," Rae said. "And then collect my reward."

"Ah," Silas grunted. He savagely cracked a larger stick in two and threw it on the fire. "You're one of those."

Rae shot him a piercing glance. "And what's that supposed to mean?"

"You are one who accepted the call to join the Youth Guard merely for the spectacular reward that is promised for those who complete the mission."

Jesse remembered again that Silas and Rae hardly knew each other. They had gone through three months of training together at the capital, of course, but from what he had heard, it was hardly a time to make friends.

"I see," Rae said coldly. "And what is your noble reason for joining the Guard, Silas?"

Silas gave a low laugh. "That is none of your concern. But, I can assure you, it's hardly noble."

Jesse moved closer to the fire. Somehow, he felt even less safe than before. He had always thought Youth Guard members were heroes who wanted to save the land from its troubles, or at least daring young men and women who joined the Guard for the adventure. Now he was beginning to doubt the truth of that ideal.

"The desert," he said, anxious to break the tension, "is one place in the kingdom that I know very little about. The few travelers I have met from District Four keep to themselves. I've heard of wandering tribes, very fierce and war-like, and of strange creatures, but only from those who have heard from others. I've never talked to anyone who has actually been there."

"Perhaps because there's little reason for anyone to journey into a desert," Silas said.

"Or because those who do never survive," Rae said darkly.

That comment cut off the rest of the conversation, and the three travelers ate their rations, some bread and salted meat from Kayne's storeroom, in silence. "We'll need to get some rest," Silas said when they had finished. "Tomorrow will be more of the same."

That gives us a lot to look forward to. Jesse bit back his complaint. He did not want to show any sign of weakness.

Silas glanced up at the clear, cloudless sky. "No rain on the way," he observed. "There would be little use in setting up the tents." He took out the blanket from his pack and used the rest as a pillow. Jesse followed his lead.

"I'll take the first watch," Rae said, standing.

"We're still a day's travel from the desert," Silas pointed out, not even opening his eyes. "There is no danger here. Go to sleep."

Rae frowned. "I'll take the first watch."

Silas, clearly having learned that it was impossible to argue with the strong-willed girl, just sighed and rolled over. "Wake me in a few hours to replace you."

Jesse pulled his blanket over himself but kept his eyes open. He had never had such an eventful day in all his life, and he was not ready to sleep yet. *I might not be able to sleep at all on this hard ground.*

He stared up at the stars, beyond the towering peaks of the mountains, and remembered the stories his father had told him about them when he was young. He could see the stars that formed Lorar, the warrior who killed the two-headed snake whose name Jesse could not remember. Marias, the first of the kings, who named the kingdom Amarias after himself. Nigel, who hunted great beasts with his falcons and hawks. Kiondra the maiden, whose singing made the very mountains melt. Jesse could almost hear her voice.

Wait, he thought, cocking his head. *I believe I can.*

But it was not a mythical heroine who sang. It was Rae. Jesse propped his head up on his elbow and squinted into the darkness. Although she stood rigidly near the edge of a cliff, hand on her sword, her soft voice floated freely across the gorge, like the most graceful of the phoenixes. The song had no words, just rich, lonely sounds that echoed quietly in the dark.

For a brief moment, Jesse considered standing and apologizing for his foolish words earlier. Then he lay back down. *She wouldn't want my apology. She doesn't want me here at all.*

That night, he dreamed of a huge red dragon, pulling Rae and Silas down into a swirling pit of sand. There was nothing he could do to save them. All he could do was beat the dragon with his staff, until he was sucked into the sand too, forever lost to the mysterious Abaktan Desert.

CHAPTER 9

Death. That was what Jesse thought of the moment he caught his first glimpse of the Abaktan Desert at the end of the second day of travel. It stretched out in front of him like a great ocean, flat and barren of life. Nothing but white sand, the color of bleached bones, for countless miles, broken only by a stray cactus or a passing vulture.

"We're going *across* that?" Jesse said doubtfully. "Is it safe?"

Rae snorted at him in contempt. Lightly, she jumped off the brown grass where they stood onto the edge of the sand. Without looking back, she strode into the desert, her boots sinking only slightly into the ground.

Silas shifted the burden on his back. "Does that answer your question?"

"I meant for anyone human," Jesse muttered. Hesitantly, he took his first step on the white sand. It did not suck him under, and no fierce creatures clawed their way out.

His staff was harder to use as a crutch in the sand, because it sank farther down than it had on level ground. Still, Silas stayed by Jesse's side, even at the slower pace. *He must feel sorry for me. Or maybe he thinks I'll get lost if he doesn't stay with me.*

Then Jesse noticed Silas' awkward steps and nearly laughed. *He really can't move any faster.* Of course, it made sense. Silas was much taller than either Jesse or Rae, and had volunteered to carry most of the equipment, including the heavy canvas tents. The imbalance in weight made him sink farther in the sand.

The sun, even as it began to dip in the sky, burned down on them harshly. Ever since they had left the mountain gorge that morning, the temperature had steadily increased. Noon had been almost unbearable.

"I studied the map this morning," Silas said. "Leden is close by."

Jesse nodded. Leden, an oasis town at the edge of the desert, would be a good place to spend the night. *Perhaps we will even get to sleep in a real bed.* He knew the king had given the Youth Guard enough gold and silver coins to supply them with whatever they might need.

"If we keep a steady pace," Silas continued, "we should reach it by nightfall."

Rae turned back. "I wouldn't be so sure about that, with you two lagging behind. Even if we walk into the night, we'll be lucky to make it halfway there."

They tried to move faster, but Rae still stayed ahead of them, walking as lightly as if she was going for an afternoon stroll.

"You should know, Jesse," Silas said as they stumbled on, "this will not be a short journey."

Jesse's heart sank. He had hoped they would be able to stay at Leden. It was the only desert town on the map. "Then where is our destination?"

"Da'armos."

Da'armos? "But…that's halfway through the Abaktan Desert," Jesse said, puzzled. "It's not even part of Amarias."

"But King Selen conquered it in the War of Palms five years ago," Silas reminded him. "At first, the Sheik…." He noticed Jesse's puzzled expression. "That's what they call their king. For a while, he sent the required tribute by caravan into District Four. But this year the payments stopped."

Jesse just stared at him. "And we're supposed to storm into enemy territory and demand this year's tribute?"

Silas nodded. "Not only that, but, as payment for the Sheik's tardiness, we are to bring back the greatest treasure of Da'armos: the Scorpion's Jewel."

Rae doubled back to join them. "They say it's set in pure gold," she said, clearly having heard all of their conversation. "No one knows what kind of jewel it is, because no Amarian has ever been permitted to see it."

"And the captain of the Youth Guard thinks we'll be able to steal it?" Jesse asked in disbelief.

"Not steal it," Rae corrected. "Demand it as tribute. We represent the king and the entire force of King Selen's army."

"Who are all busy fighting on the Northern Waste," Jesse pointed out.

"Youth Guard missions are supposed to be a challenge," Silas said, shrugging.

Jesse stared at him. "Challenging is getting across this desert alive in the first place. This is more than challenging. Think about what will happen when three dirty, scrawny—"

"Excuse me," Rae interrupted, sounding indignant. "I, for one, intend to be presentable. And I would hardly consider Silas scrawny."

"Fine," Jesse said. "One dirty, scrawny boy, and two clean, only slightly more impressive Youth Guard members, stumble into a foreign land, knowing none of the language. They are from the nation that just conquered Da'armos and killed hundreds of the Da'armon people. Then they storm into the throne room and demand that the Sheik give them tribute for their king and also, the greatest treasure of the kingdom."

He paused for breath. "Do you want to know what happens to those three?"

"No," Rae said flatly.

"Yes," Silas said at the same time. She gave him a look, and he shrugged. "It was just getting interesting."

"They get thrown into prison for the rest of their miserable lives," Jesse said triumphantly. "Or, much more likely, their heads are cut off and displayed at the city gates. That's not challenging. That's impossible."

"Fine," Rae shot back. "Then turn back." She pointed to the south, where Jesse could still see the peaks of the Suspicion Mountains. "You know the way."

For a moment, Jesse felt like accepting her challenge, turning away and going back to the relative safety of the mountains. Then he remembered Parvel. *I made a promise.*

"I only wanted to point out that our mission won't be as easy as you both seem to think," Jesse said, continuing on. "It almost seems like they *want* us to die."

"You may remember that not many Youth Guard members survive," Silas said pointedly. "This is why." Then he sighed. "Don't worry, Jesse. It may take a week to reach Da'armos on foot. We will have time to consider our strategy."

"Excellent," Jesse said cheerfully, "we'll have time to *plan* our destruction. Or, I suppose, if Rae has her way, we won't do any planning at all, but just stumble blindly into our own deaths."

Rae glared at him for that, but Silas was not listening. His eyes were focused on a point in the distance. "What is that?" he asked sharply, pointing to the east.

From a distance, it looked like a great swarm of gnats, so vast that it blocked out the sun. *But no gnats create that kind of wind.* Jesse thought back to what he had heard about the Abaktan Desert, and his heart beat faster as he realized what they were seeing. *Sandstorm.*

For a moment, all three stood motionless, staring at the wall of sand that was whipping toward them.

Silas was the first to jerk his eyes away. "To the rocks!" he called, pointing to a pile of pale stones a distance away. "They will shield us!"

If we can get there before the sandstorm does. Jesse tried to run, beating the ground frantically with his staff, but Silas and Rae were soon ahead of him.

He glanced over his shoulder only once. What he saw terrified him so much that he determined never to look again.

The whirlwind literally picked up the hills and dunes and spun their contents in a deadly blur. The scrawny cacti in the distance were engulfed in seconds.

And we'll be next.

For the first time in his life, Jesse prayed, almost without thinking. *God, if you're out there, help us!*

A glance in front of him told Jesse that the rocks were still far away—too far, he knew. *But what else can we do?* he thought in desperation. *We can't just lie down and die.*

That's it!

"Silas!" Jesse shouted, using all the energy he had left to be heard over the wind. It was growing louder as the sandstorm came closer.

Silas, still running, turned back. He must have seen how quickly the storm was coming, because his eyes widened. "The tents!" Jesse shouted, pointing at the pack Silas carried. Jesse hoped he understood, because he had no time to explain.

For a moment, Silas hesitated. Then he dropped to the ground and began digging through the pack, looking for the tent.

Rae, not realizing what was happening, was still running. *Even she won't reach the rocks in time.*

Jesse took a deep breath to call for Rae. Instantly, he coughed violently, as the first of the flying sand particles invaded his lungs. He pulled a blanket from his pack and wrapped it around the bottom part of his face.

"Rae!" he shouted, running after her as fast as he could, ignoring the pain in his crippled leg.

She did not even turn.

"Rae!" Jesse shouted again. The sandstorm was upon them now, and Jesse had to squint to keep his eyes from the blowing sand. "Rae!"

Then he saw her. She had crumpled to the ground, shielding her face with her arms. He lunged forward the last few steps and tried to speak to her. The wind picked up his words and drove them deeper into the desert.

"Come on!" Jesse shouted, grabbing Rae's arm. She cried out, then immediately spat, trying to get rid of the sand that had entered her mouth.

This time, at least, Rae was not strong enough to help herself. And that meant Jesse had to do something to save her—to save both of them.

Jesse didn't waste any time. He pulled her to her feet and yanked her forward. The blowing sand made it impossible to see anything. He had no idea where he was going. There was nothing but wind and sand and heat. *And death. Just like I knew there would be.*

Then, faintly, Jesse heard Silas' voice shouting at the top of his lungs. No words, just a constant cry. He dragged Rae in the direction of that cry, stumbling against the wind. Once the cry grew louder, he eased his eyes open a crack.

Silas was on his knees in the sand, his eyes closed and hands tightly gripping the tent. The large slab of canvas flapped crazily in the wind. *There is nothing to anchor it,* Jesse realized, his mind struggling to come up with a plan.

"Get underneath," he ordered Rae, his voice muffled through the blanket. "Everyone grab a corner."

Whether or not they heard him, Silas and Rae seemed

to understand what to do. They crouched together, wrapping themselves in the tent. Jesse was nearly twisted backwards, trying to hold down one side of the canvas with his knees and grasping a corner with each hand.

Although they were protected from the sting of the blowing sand, the wind still beat against the canvas. *Don't move,* Jesse commanded himself. *If you topple over, the tent will too.*

It was dark in the tent. Once, Jesse felt himself falling forward. He bumped into Silas, but Silas did not so much as flinch. *He is saving us,* Jesse realized. Although he and Rae were swayed about with the wind, Silas was like a pillar under the Dell River bridge: stable and unmoving.

Unable to blow them away, the sandstorm settled instead for burying them alive. Jesse felt the pressure as sand began to build up around them. "Keep as much air as possible," he ordered, trying to expand the tent against the push of the sand.

Playing with death. Just like Parvel said. Jesse pushed the thought away and kept holding up the tent, trying not to breathe too deeply.

Jesse had no idea how long the sandstorm went on. Each beat of his heart seemed to take hours, but logic told him they had been under the canvas for a much shorter time. Once they were completely covered in sand—their bodies holding up only small pockets of air—he could no longer hear the howling wind.

It may be too soon to try to dig out. That would be the worst—to abandon their safe place and find that the storm still continued above. *But before long, we will not be able to breathe.*

Even now, Jesse could hear the sharp, uneven breathing of his two companions. They would not be able to last long.

When the breathing quieted Jesse knew they must move. He could feel his heart rate begin to slow. "We have to stand together," he said, his words sounding tired, even to his own ears, "and push up."

"Now," Silas ordered. Slowly, they stood from their uncomfortable crouch, pushing the canvas up with them.

It did not break through.

Jesse felt panic shoot through him. *We could be underneath a mountain of sand. We'll never reach the surface!*

The sand around them was quickly sliding into the space they had opened by standing, burying their precious remaining air, and Jesse took one last gasping breath.

Silas pushed upward against the sand, digging in the direction they believed was up. Jesse joined him, closing his eyes as sand began to press against them. Blindly, he clawed at the sand. Once, Jesse felt a stab of pain as a hand slashed at his arm by mistake.

And then Jesse's hand felt something other than the grit of sand. *Air.*

His head came next, and he sputtered and gasped like a drowning man pulled out of a river. Slowly, he wriggled his way out of the dune and swiped the sand away from his face.

Nearby, Rae was helping Silas to his feet. *She tried to save Silas first,* he thought bitterly, coughing the sand from his lungs. Then he shook his head. *She had no way of knowing who she was pulling from the sand.*

With a shake of his head, Jesse tried to get the sand out of his hair. It was useless, he knew. Sand was everywhere: in his ears, his clothes, his supplies....

The supplies! Just to make sure, Jesse reached to his back. Sure enough, no pack was strapped there. "Silas!" he said, crawling over to him. "The supplies! I...."

Rae shook her head. "Mine too," she said. "We'll dig them out in the morning."

"But...what if there's another storm?"

"I have my pack," Silas said, setting it down. His voice was raw, either from the sand or from shouting. "We will have enough for tonight. And we have the canvas."

"Besides," Rae said quietly, "I don't think we could last through another storm." Jesse had never before seen her so subdued. *Perhaps the sand rubbed away her layer of bluster.*

Jesse took a quick look around. Even in the dark, he could tell the landscape had been entirely changed. Only the rocks in the distance, barely poking out of the newly created dune, proved that they were in the same part of the desert. Cacti had popped up where they had not been before; old ones had disappeared.

"We should not have survived that," Silas stated, without any emotion.

A quick shiver went down Jesse's spine. He knew Silas was right. He had never heard of anyone living through a sandstorm. *Perhaps God was listening after all.*

No, he decided, shaking his head. *My quick thinking saved us, and nothing more.*

Silas passed around his skin of water, and they each washed their mouths out, then took a long drink. Too exhausted to say more, they curled up in the sand. *We will not sleep in Leden tonight.*

Jesse shivered and pulled his blanket over him. With the sun gone, the night was suddenly cold. As he closed his eyes, Jesse felt the irritating, ever-present scrape of sand against his skin and found it hard to sleep.

Worse, everything was silent. *Deathly silent.*

CHAPTER 10

Noon in the desert. The sun blazed mercilessly on the three travelers, mocking their slow progress. Jesse felt ready to fall to the ground and die. At least then there would be some relief from the heat, the pain of his crippled leg and sore body, and the endless monotony of the white sand in front of him.

They had started out well. After digging out what remained of their supplies, they had journeyed in the direction that Silas assured them was east, toward Leden. No one could find Jesse's water skin, and they decided to leave it behind rather than spend more time searching.

It was a great loss, they soon learned. Between the hard travel and the constant release of fluids through sweating, they needed much more water than they had planned. Soon, Silas' water skin was empty, and Rae's only half full. *It might be enough to last us until nightfall, if we conserve. But what then?*

"Rest," Silas called out. They had all been trying to use as few words as possible. Their mouths were dry, and conversation wasted precious moisture.

Rae looked the worst, although she did not complain. Her lips were cracked, and she moved stiffly, as if putting one foot in front of the other required great effort. Silas had insisted she drape a cloth over her head to protect her fair skin from the burning sun, but her pale cheeks had already turned scarlet red.

Jesse wished he had brought some of Kayne's remedy for burnt skin. Then again, his pack already felt heavy enough to pull him deep down in the sand. Each step was a fight, and he was glad to slump down to rest.

"I'll look ahead," Rae said, walking toward the rocks ahead of them. She was still their scout, scanning for any sign of civilization, but her ventures had become less and less frequent as the day dragged on.

"We should have reached Leden long ago," Silas muttered heavily.

"The sandstorm," Jesse said. "It changed everything. We don't even know where we are anymore."

There was certainly nothing around him to look at. Everything was hot and white and endless. He fingered the tortoise high on the staff. The upraised ridges on its shell reminded Jesse of all the times he and Eli had caught tortoises on the banks of the Dell River. *The river—all that water, gushing over the rocks....*

Jesse shook his head. *Just think about the tortoise.* For determination, Kayne had said. *Well, determination would serve me well here.*

The wooden tortoise gave Jesse an idea. "Silas," he said. The older boy was studying the map, and barely looked up at Jesse's words. "I've heard about desert tortoises who eat the buds of a cactus to survive. It's a source of water for them."

Silas' face had frozen.

"We haven't seen many cacti," Jesse continued, starting to feel a little bit of hope, "but if we…."

"Don't move," Silas ordered, interrupting. His voice was quiet, but the deadly seriousness in it made Jesse obey instantly. He did not blink and tried not to breathe.

Silas carefully reached back to his quiver of arrows, but instead of fitting one to his bow, he struck forward with it, plunging the arrow into the ground by Jesse's leg.

Slowly, Jesse looked down. There, pinned to the ground, was a scorpion, larger than Jesse's hand. It had been only inches away from his unprotected leg.

"Thank you," Jesse stammered out.

Silas nodded. "Thank you for yesterday. You saved all of our lives."

Although he did not want to, Jesse found himself looking back at the dead scorpion. *Probably about to strike*, he thought. *Good thing Silas struck first.*

Then Jesse groaned. Beside the scorpion, the sand was beginning to move. He barely had time to jerk away. *Not another one!*

The sand beside the scorpion caved in, leaving behind a small hole. An insect crawled out of the hole with a high-pitched, whining hum. It shook sand off its large, translucent wings and flew into the air.

Jesse stared at it in fascination. The insect bore a slight resemblance to the locusts he had known from Mir, but it was three times as big as any locust he had ever seen before. *And three times as ugly.* Sickly yellowish skin flaked over the bony spines of the creature, and its legs stuck out at odd angles.

The insect swooped toward him, and Jesse scurried back in the sand. But the locust-creature did not seem to be interested in him at all. Instead, it landed on the scorpion and began tearing it to pieces, as if it was starving.

Behind them, Rae gave a little shriek. She had come back and was holding the open water skin. The locust-creature veered toward her side, and she stumbled forward, spilling some of their precious water. The locust-creature gave a hiss of agony the moment the water touched it. Suddenly, it whirred into a frenzy, spinning and flying through the air so quickly it became a dark blur.

"Stay back," Silas shouted, as if he needed to warn them. Rae dropped to the sand, as the locust-creature continued its mad spiral. Once, it buzzed past Jesse's ear, and he cringed. The noise it made in its panic sounded like an unearthly scream.

Then, suddenly, it fell to the sand and lay there, lifeless.

"What *is* it?" Rae asked, recovering quickly. She stood and brushed the sand from her clothes.

"Dead, I think," Silas said, eying it warily. "The water killed it."

"No, I don't think so," Jesse said, staring down at it.

All of a sudden, the locust-creature twitched, and Rae gave a startled jerk. Jesse had to bite his lip to keep from laughing. *Rae, boldest of warriors, is afraid of an insect.* He knew that if he were to make that observation out loud, it would be his last.

"Good fortune to you, young travelers," a voice called.

Rae turned around so quickly she kicked sand on Jesse's feet. More slowly, Jesse leaned against his staff and turned to face a comical looking man on a large, ugly camel. He wore a bright red robe and a white cloth around his head, held in place by a crooked silver band. The camel lurched from side to side like a furry sailing ship as the man urged it forward.

"Who are you?" Rae demanded, stepping forward, as if she would attack the beast of a camel at the slightest hint of threat.

The man dismounted and led his camel toward them. "I am Samariyosin," he said, giving a mocking half-bow. "Trader and merchant of goods between Amarias and Da'armos."

Da'armos. Samariyosin knew where Da'armos was. More importantly, he probably also knew where he was now.

Jesse studied him carefully. He was short and had clearly seen many years of the harsh desert wind. His robe was dirty and soaked with sweat. His eyes, deep within the wrinkles of his weather-beaten face, were sharp and intelligent, but not threatening. *We don't need to be afraid of him,* Jesse decided.

"That, at least, explains why I am here in the desert," Samariyosin continued, "but why are you three alone, young, unprotected and so far from any village?"

"That's our concern," Rae snapped.

Very good, Rae. Offend the only guide we have.

"We represent the king of Amarias," Silas said, giving Rae a cautioning glance. "We are traveling to Da'armos to speak to the Sheik."

"Ah," said Samariyosin, his eyes widening slightly. "Then I would do well to wish you good fortune, brave young travelers. Although it appears you have good fortune enough."

He was looking at the remains of the scorpion and the body of the locust-creature on the ground. "The scorpions are deadly, you know."

"And the locust?" Jesse asked, pointing to the other creature on the ground, still twitching. He had been too afraid to come close enough to crush it.

"A kalthara," Samariyosin said with a nod. "They only attack something larger than themselves if they smell blood or decay." He grinned, his teeth white against tan skin. "In Da'armon, kalthara means 'vulture insect.'"

A fitting name, Jesse thought in disgust.

"When the water touched it, why did it...." Silas couldn't seem to think of a fitting word to describe the panicked frenzy of the kalthara.

"The kalthara can stay alive for months without drinking anything," Samariyosin explained. "It has a protective layer of mucus covering its body. The water eats away at it. Very painful."

Jesse stared at the insect, still twitching on the sand. "I suppose so."

"As soon as his wings dry, he'll be up and flying again," Samariyosin said casually. He dismounted from the camel, sandaled feet sinking into the sand. "Off to terrorize the people of Da'armos. That's where the rest are at this time of year. I'm surprised this one is so far from the pod."

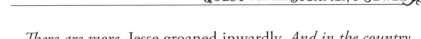

There are more, Jesse groaned inwardly. *And in the country we are traveling to.*

"Terrible creatures, kaltharas," Samariyosin continued, picking up the locust between two fingers. It writhed in his grasp, its chirping hiss sending a shiver down Jesse's spine. He watched in horror as Samariyosin opened his mouth and tossed the locust in. It crunched as he bit down.

He wiped his mouth calmly, not noticing the stares of the three travelers. "But they make for excellent eating."

CHAPTER 11

Ten guards traveled with Samariyosin's caravan, huge and imposing men armed with enough swords and bows to supply a detachment of the Amarian army.

And, yet, as Jesse, Silas, Rae, and Samariyosin himself crouched by a small fire at the edge of the camp, no guards protected them from any desert bandits who might ambush them.

As soon as Jesse turned around and scanned the camp, he knew why. Several dark figures were clustered around the tent that held the trading goods. *Ah. I suppose that means we're not worth as much as spices and woven cloth.*

It was not a comforting thought, especially since night had fallen, and Samariyosin had told them that Nalatid, the oasis town nearby, was known as a haven for rogues and thieves.

"Nalatid is the largest oasis in the Abaktan Desert, and the closest to the Da'armon border," Samariyosin said, throwing more chips on the fire. He had explained earlier that they collected the dung from their camels, dried it, and used it in place of firewood, which was scarce in the desert. "We'll be at the Da'armon capital by tomorrow afternoon."

After another day of travel through the desert, that was welcome news. Jesse wasn't quite as sore as he had been the first night. Riding on a camel was much easier than walking, even if the padded saddle wasn't quite enough to make the bumpy journey comfortable.

"Thank you for letting us travel with your caravan," Silas said politely, as one of Samariyosin's servants handed him a bowl of stew.

"It was nothing," Samariyosin said dismissively, waving away the thanks with a flutter of his long-sleeved robe.

That, at least, was true. Jesse was fairly sure that Samariyosin would have left them standing there if Rae hadn't mentioned the silver coins she carried, coins she would give to someone who would guide them to Da'armos. Samariyosin had been only too willing to volunteer.

The servant, one of many traveling with Samariyosin's caravan, gave Jesse his bowl. It was still hot, and Jesse balanced it on the edge of his fingertips. That, at least, gave him an excuse not to start eating yet. In the dark, Jesse couldn't identify what was in it. He decided to let Silas or Rae take the first sip.

Rae seemed to have other things on her mind. "How is it that you speak Amarian and Da'armon?" she asked Samariyosin.

"Ah," Samariyosin said, nodding. "An excellent question. I am, as you would say, a half-breed. My father was a trader also, born in the capital of Da'armos. He met my mother, one of your own kind, on one of his journeys. This was before the War of Palms, of course, when such marriages were not forbidden. They taught me both languages, both sets of customs."

He tilted his head back and took a gulp of soup. Jesse noticed that Silas did the same, although with a bit more caution. When he didn't wince, spit into the fire, or drop dead, Jesse picked up his own bowl, finally realizing how hungry he really was.

Jesse tried hard not to think about the kaltharas while he ate the stew. He also tried not to think of the fuel that was used in the fire it had been cooked over. With those things out of his mind, the stew was actually quite good. A little spicy, maybe, but filling. *And, more importantly, there's nothing crunchy in it.*

Silas set his bowl down and looked intently at Samariyosin from across the fire. "I have heard that some members of the movement we in Amarias call the Rebellion, cross the border of Da'armos for safety," he said. "Is this true?"

Samariyosin laughed. "I can assure you that it is not. No citizen of Amarias is welcome in Da'armos. If any of the Rebellion sought shelter here, they would no doubt be killed instantly."

"Good," Silas said with satisfaction. "It's no more than they deserve."

"Why do you hate them so much?" Rae asked him, sipping some of her own soup. "What they do is foolish, but these are desperate times. Many are without food, and maybe they feel like they have nowhere else to turn."

"I have no use for lawlessness," Silas snapped, refusing to look at her. "They are nothing more than common criminals."

Rae just shrugged. "At least they're taking some sort of action rather than letting their families starve. The king clearly isn't looking out for us. I say it's every person for himself."

This earned her a cutting glare from Silas. "Yes," he said coldly. "I forgot you are a mercenary, selling your loyalty to the highest bidder."

For a moment, there was silence around the fire. Then Samariyosin, clearly uncomfortable, changed the subject. "Now," he said, setting his bowl down by the fire to keep it warm, "I have a question for you. The Sheik does not grant audiences lightly. How is it that three young people wish to speak to the ruler of the land?"

Jesse glanced at Silas, who gave a strong shake of his head. Apparently Rae wasn't watching, because before Silas could cut her off, she answered Samariyosin's question with a question of her own. "What can you tell us about the Scorpion's Jewel?"

In the firelight, Jesse could see confusion flicker across the old man's face. Then he grinned. "Ah, you mean the obidhala," he said. "I forgot the name given it by foreigners."

Since Silas seemed to be too busy glaring at Rae to speak up, Jesse asked, "Is it true that it is the greatest treasure of Da'armos?"

"Yes. Given by the gods, or so it is said. It comes with a powerful curse for any who would try to harm the king or his people."

Wonderful. Although Jesse did not believe the stories about the obidhala, as Samariyosin called it, he also knew the treasure would be well-guarded. *Which is not good for us.*

"Why do you ask?" Samariyosin said casually, draining the last of his stew. He wiped his mouth on the corner of his headdress.

Silas didn't hesitate. "We have heard it has some power to curse the king of our country. King Selen sent us to investigate these rumors."

"Of course." Samariyosin nodded. Somehow, Jesse knew he didn't believe them, but he seemed content to accept their false answer. "I can assure you, though, that the obidhala is harmless. The curse is mere legend. How else would you explain Da'armos' defeat in the War of Palms?"

"Just the same," Rae said, "we will speak to the Sheik about it."

Before Samariyosin could ask any further questions, one of the armed guards hurried up to him. He said something to the merchant in Da'armon.

"Amarian Patrol members," Samariyosin muttered under his breath, spitting contemptuously in the sand. "They ask for my papers every time I pass through a town. That is the problem with being a half-breed: you are not fully trusted by either side."

He stood slowly and edged away from the fire, bowing slightly to them. "You will have to excuse me, young guests. I will be back with you soon."

Jesse watched him as he made his way to the other side

of the camp, where three men were waiting in the shadows beyond the main tent.

"Why did you ask him about the Scorpion's Jewel?" Silas demanded, turning to Rae. "I thought we had agreed never to speak of our mission."

"How do you expect us to accomplish our mission if we don't know anything about the territory we're entering or the object we need to bring back?" Rae took one last sip of soup and delicately wiped her mouth on her sleeve. "I was just gathering information."

Will they ever stop bickering? Jesse guessed the answer was no, so he changed the subject. "What do you think of our host?"

Silas shook his head hard. "I can't wait to be rid of him. He doesn't seem trustworthy. No merchant could become this rich by honest means."

Rae shrugged. "Dishonest or not, he knows the way to Da'armos. And it will be useful to have a translator with us when we get there."

"And what of the Scorpion's Jewel?" Silas asked. "Do you have any plan to secure this obidhala that he spoke of?"

"No," Rae admitted. "Do you?"

"I hoped we would be able to plan on the journey tomorrow. Only Samariyosin seems to speak Amarian, and he will be at the head of the caravan. It may be that…."

"Shh," Rae hissed, jerking her head toward the tents, "he's coming back."

Samariyosin was indeed scurrying his way across the sand. As he came back into the firelight, Jesse noticed how old and tired he looked. "It is late," Samariyosin said, as if reading Jesse's mind. "I am sure you must be weary from your journey."

Rae nodded and stood, brushing the sand from her tunic. "It's been a long day."

"I could use some rest," Silas agreed.

Jesse stayed where he was. He was used to staying up late, serving guests at the inn. Though he was tired, he was excited too, and a bit frightened, neither of which would be good for going to sleep. *So close to Da'armos. And then what?*

"I've had three more tents prepared already." Samariyosin nodded and clapped his hands twice, and two of the light-robed servants seemed to appear out of the darkness at his side. He rattled off a string of commands, and each one escorted Rae and Silas away. Jesse noticed they were taken in opposite directions, and he wondered if that had been part of Samariyosin's instructions.

Jesse shook his head. "If you don't mind, I'd like to stay up a little while longer." Though they were still in Amarias, there was no curfew in the desert. Jesse enjoyed being out under the stars, especially since night was the only endurable part of the day, when the sun did not burn at his back.

"Your two friends seem to be more inclined to talk than you," Samariyosin said. "I don't even know your name."

"My name is Jesse," he said.

"Ah," Samariyosin said. "What does it mean?"

Jesse blinked. "Nothing. Nothing that I know of, at least."

"Ah. I forgot. You are an Amarian," Samariyosin said.

Jesse was not quite sure what that meant, and it must have showed on his face. "Here in Da'armos, names have great meaning," Samariyosin explained. "Mine means, 'He who has no fear of the night terrors.'"

"Samariyosin," Jesse said thoughtfully. "It's a long name, isn't it?"

He shrugged. "All of my people have long names."

"Do you mind if I call you Sam?"

Samariyosin frowned, and Jesse was afraid he had offended him. "Sam has no meaning in Da'armon."

"How about Samar, then?" Jesse tried. "I would think that 'He who has no fear' is far more impressive. And much easier to pronounce."

Samariyosin's leathery face broke into a grin. "That it is, young Jesse. You may call me Samar if you like."

Tilting his head back, Jesse looked up at the stars. Once again, Jesse was amazed at their beauty. "You could never count them all," he mumbled to himself.

"Marakondanset," Samar said, offhandedly. "It was my father's name, meaning, 'Servant of the Numberer of the stars.' That is one of the titles the people of Da'armos give their god of justice and the afterlife."

Justice. The word made Jesse think of Parvel. "Do you believe in God, Samar?"

"I have never given it much thought," Samar said, after thinking for a few seconds. He too looked up at the stars. "Perhaps there is a Being of sorts who made all of it. How else would you explain the stars?"

Jesse just grunted. It was not what he wanted to hear.

"But," Samar added, "in all my years, I have never seen evidence of any sort of personal God, one who listens." He paused, threw more chips on the fire. "Then again, I have never made any attempt to find one either. Never saw the need."

Then perhaps that is why you've never heard Him. Jesse shook his head to rid it of Parvel's words. He wanted to forget the whole business, but everywhere he turned, it seemed, something would remind him of Parvel and his God.

They fell back into a comfortable silence. Looking at Samar, Jesse remembered all the guests at his uncle's inn. The merchants and traders especially, whether they traveled by land or sea, had the look that Jesse saw in Samar's face now. It was the lonely look of someone who has no one to talk to. Those were the people, Jesse knew, who told the best stories of all.

"Samar," Jesse began, "traveling around the desert with a caravan this large, you must have encountered some trouble in your days."

"Of course," Samar said, a deep laugh bubbling up like water from the oasis. "Of course I have, young Jesse." Then he stared into the fire, lost in his memories. "But surely you don't wish to hear an old man babble."

In that moment, instead of a blustering man with a dozen servants at his command and a caravan of fine goods, Jesse saw a lonely old man with no family and no close friends. "I do," he said simply.

Samar's deep-set eyes seemed to brighten, and he leaned back in the sand. "I remember it as if it was yesterday, the day the Amarian soldiers thought I was a spy for Da'armos...."

An hour later, Jesse crept to his tent, a small linen cloth pegged to the ground near the edge of the oasis, his mind full of tales of betrayal, pursuit, and adventure. He must have fallen asleep as soon as he lay on the mat, because the next thing he remembered was someone shaking him. He almost cried out, then stopped himself.

"Jesse," an urgent voice whispered. "You must get up at once."

Samar. But it can't be morning yet, can it?

The old man crouched above him, and he was clearly agitated for some reason. He splashed some cold water on Jesse's face, making him gasp slightly. "Make haste," he whispered again. "Grab your belongings. You and your friends must leave here at once."

"What?" Jesse muttered sleepily. It was an easy thing to gather his possessions: they were right where he had laid them before falling asleep. He took his walking stick, leaning against the side of the tent. "Why? What's happening?"

Samar grabbed his arm and dragged him out of the tent. "Not a word, not a sound," he said. "The camels are packed and waiting, but we must hurry."

"Stop," Jesse commanded in a whisper, and Samar did, staring back at him with wide, frightened eyes. "Please, Samar, I need to know what is happening."

"I could not do it," Samar whispered hoarsely. "Though it may cost me my life, I could not do it."

"Do what?"

Samar took a deep breath, which seemed to calm him down some. "The Patrol members who came earlier…they are assassins who are coming to kill you. I do not know why. I do not know what you have done. All they asked is that I let it happen. But I could not do it."

There would be time for more explanation later. "I'll wake Rae," Jesse said. "You get Silas." Jesse practically ran to Rae's tent. "Rae!" he hissed. "It's Jesse."

"Be grateful that you identified yourself," Rae growled from the dark. "I nearly stabbed you."

That made Jesse take a step back. "Rae, our lives are in danger. Get up, grab your things, and follow me."

Outside the tent, Samar was waiting with Silas. "Come," Samar said, motioning them forward. He carried a wicker basket lashed to his back, the kind that hung from the saddles of the camels, and a large water skin. "We must go on foot now."

"Where are we going?" Jesse asked.

"No more questions," Samar insisted. "Just follow." He shoved a thick palm branch at Silas. "You—wipe out our tracks as we walk. I fear the patrol members are already nearby, but if they are not, we will not leave them a trail."

Jesse remembered that trick from one of Samar's stories. *But I never thought I'd be in one of them.*

"Do not look back, and move silently," Samar advised them. *"Riangen da'ede.* 'Even the sand dunes have eyes.'"

Someone is watching us? But why?

Old as he was, fear had apparently made Samar quicker than his years. He hurried through the camp and over the hills near the oasis. Even with the use of his walking stick, it was hard for Jesse to keep his pace.

The moon on the white sand made it easy for Jesse to see where he was going. *Which means it will be equally easy for anyone to see us.* The thought made him hurry to the top of the first of the hills.

"The Patrol did not know of the smugglers' pits when I came last year," Samar said, leading the way. "Let us hope that they have not learned of them since then."

Even though Samar had warned him several times not to turn back, Jesse took one last look at the camp from the top of the hill.

There, three men with swords hacked their way into his tent.

CHAPTER 12

The pit, a gaping hole in the ground, was so deep Jesse could not see its bottom. There was nothing but blackness below, and Jesse almost felt that he would be sucked in if he stood too close.

"I suppose you're going to ask us to jump in," he guessed, trying to prepare himself for the worst.

Samar snorted a laugh. "Hardly. You would contaminate the water supply. These cisterns are used by shepherds and nomads. I'm sure they'd rather you didn't waste what little water we can store in these parts. And," he added, almost as an afterthought, "it would be a very long fall."

"If there's water below," Rae said, a worried frown creasing her face, "then how can we hide? I don't know how to swim."

"I used to," Jesse said. "But now, with one good leg, I can only stay above water for a few minutes."

Samar waved at them impatiently. "Just watch." He crouched down beside the pit and reached down inside of it. "It should be here," he said, groping around in the darkness.

Silas lurched forward to grab the old man's shoulders as he started to tip.

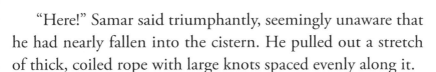

"Here!" Samar said triumphantly, seemingly unaware that he had nearly fallen into the cistern. He pulled out a stretch of thick, coiled rope with large knots spaced evenly along it.

"So, we're all going to hang from the rope and wait until the Patrol members pass by," Rae suggested, raising an eyebrow.

"I'll take my chances and hide myself in the sand," Jesse said immediately.

Rae shuddered. "Not me. Never again. It felt like I was being buried alive."

"If you don't stop talking, you will be buried *dead* in a few moments," Samar snapped. They stopped talking. "Climb down the rope into the cistern. At the end of the rope, you should find a ladder to your left."

"Should?" Jesse asked pointedly.

Samar ignored him. "The ladder leads to a cavern dug into the side of the cistern. There is enough room for all of us." He glanced back over the hills. "Now, hurry, before the Patrol finds us here!"

"I'll go first," Silas said. "I'll be able to help the rest of you." Without wasting another second, he grabbed the top of the rope and slid into the cistern.

The rope held.

Jesse breathed a sigh of relief. If it could hold Silas, it would hold any of them.

"You next," Samar said to Rae. "I will go last."

Rae is supposed to climb while Silas is still on the rope? "I don't know if...." But Rae was already edging into the darkness of the cistern.

Jesse knew that he was next, and he willed his hands to stop sweating. He wondered if he would be able to climb. Perhaps Silas and Rae had been through exercises like this in their training, but since the accident, all he had done was help with farm chores and clean tables.

Relax, he told himself. *It will be just like the bridge. You can do it.*

"Now you, Jesse," Samar said. Jesse glanced at the walking stick in his hand, and Samar followed his gaze.

"Leave it," Samar advised. "We'll be back up eventually. Bury it in the sand."

"Won't the assassins find it and know we're here?"

Samar's weather-beaten face was grim. "If they're that close, they'll find us too. Now, hurry."

Jesse started to bury the stick, then stopped. "No. I'll take it down myself."

"You'll never make it with one hand." Samar sighed, then snatched it from him. "Here." He thrust the walking stick into a loop of his belt that held his sword, money pouch, and other valuables. Cinched tightly against his waist, the staff barely moved. "Now go."

As soon as he crouched down on the ground, Jesse knew that the hardest part would not be the climb: it would be the first drop into the darkness. His mouth was as dry as the desert around them as he began to climb down.

It was dark in the cistern, but cool, a nice change from the hot, dry night. Jesse had little time to enjoy it, however. Since only one leg was strong enough to support him, almost all of his weight rested on his arms. He clung to the first knot for a few seconds, then loosened his grip and slid to the next. Each drop made his stomach turn over. *I must not vomit into the cistern,* he thought. *The shepherds and nomads wouldn't appreciate that at all.*

"Eight knots," Silas called up. *He must have reached the ladder.* Jesse had just reached the fourth knot, and already his arms were trembling. A bit of dirt fell from above him. *Samar must be beginning the climb.*

Jesse grasped at the rope with his good leg, trying to give his arms a rest, but it was no use. "I'm not going to make it," he gasped, already out of breath.

"Keep coming," Silas said, from below him somewhere.

He doesn't understand! Jesse loosened his grip again, slid to the next knot. This time it was harder to tighten his grip again. One hand fell away, and he jerked it back again.

"Look up, Jesse," Samar said.

In the dark, Jesse could barely make out the old man's hand, reaching down toward him. He tried to grab it.

No! As soon as Jesse let go with one hand, the other lost its grip on the rope, and he felt himself falling.

Then a jolt knocked the breath out of him. Hard stone wall, but no water. Someone was holding onto him with a grip like an iron clamp.

A voice was shouting in pain, and Jesse joined it. He opened his eyes. Everything was blurry.

He blinked. *The ladder.* He reached out, grabbed the rung in front of him. The shouting stopped, the iron grip relaxed. For the first time, Jesse realized that it was Rae who had grabbed him, who had held him and kept him from plunging into the water below.

"Go," she said, pointing down.

Jesse climbed the ladder, which was really just a set of iron rungs welded onto the stone wall of the cistern. They looked old enough to make him nervous.

Three rungs later, Jesse saw a gash of darkness in the wall, like a giant black stain on a dark gray blanket. *The cave.*

Silas, standing in the opening, helped him jump from the ladder to the rocky ledge. Rae followed soon after, and Samar after her. They all stayed on the edge of the cave, almost as if they were afraid to go any deeper.

Samar shoved the walking stick at Jesse, and he clung to it, the familiar wood giving him a bit more confidence. Then Samar felt along the side of the cave. "There ought to be…ah!" he said with satisfaction, pulling a torch from the darkness. "And some flint on the ledge below. Just like I left it last year."

With a swift and practiced motion, he lit the torch. It provided only a dim light, but it was better than the darkness.

"Are you sure we should start a fire?" Silas pointed out. "The Patrol members might see the light or the smoke."

Samar grunted. "With all the noise we made, if they were anywhere nearby, they will find us anyway." Jesse looked at the ground, ashamed. "Besides, we will need it, at least for a little while."

Jesse picked up his staff as Samar led the way deeper into the cave. "This is the largest of the smugglers' pits," he said, holding the torch in front of him. It was barely higher than Silas's head, but big enough to hold at least a dozen men.

"It is most often a drop-off place for stolen goods, used to hide them from the Patrol of Nalatid, but sometimes smugglers with a price on their heads hide here until the king's men stop looking for them."

Jesse looked around the cave. From the gouges on the wall, it appeared to be hand-carved. *It must have taken years,* he marveled.

He was trying to figure out how high they must be above the cistern's water level when he saw something move to his right. In the shadows of the cave, Jesse could see the coiled form of a snake behind one of the rocks on the cave floor.

Silas, next to Jesse, saw it too. He shouted and jerked back, shoving Jesse with him.

It was not a good thing to do. The snake reared back to strike.

Without thinking, Jesse hit it with his staff, dashing it against the stone wall. It appeared dazed for a moment, then hissed loudly.

I've got one shot, Jesse thought with desperation. At the same time, he lunged forward with his staff, slamming it to the ground with all his might. The hissing stopped.

Jesse refused to look down, and instead turned back to Samar, Rae, and Silas, trying to calm his quickly beating heart.

"Thank you," Silas said, lowering his bow. He had not yet fitted an arrow to it. "I wouldn't have made it in time."

"And that" Samar said grimly, "is why we needed the torch. Pit vipers, we call them. I didn't want to worry you by telling you."

"Thank you for your consideration," Rae said sarcastically.

"I'm much less worried now."

"They never stay in groups," Samar assured her. "Very territorial. We won't find anymore tonight." Still, Jesse noticed that he made a careful check of the cave with the torch.

"Well," Silas said with a shrug, "we might as well get comfortable."

As if that's possible in a cavern made of solid rock. "Try the far wall," Samar suggested, seeming to read his mind. "The original builders—I was one of them—made grooves in the stone for just such occasions."

Jesse didn't understand what he was talking about until he examined the far wall more closely. Sure enough, there were large, deep indentations in the stone, rubbed smooth by years of use, and large enough to cradle the back of a man sitting in them. Although he was smaller than those for whom the grooves were designed, they were fairly comfortable.

Silas did the same, spreading the blanket from his pack over his lap. Rae chose instead to curl into a small ball at the side of the cave, using her pack as a pillow. As he leaned against the cold stone, Jesse realized all at once how tired he was.

"You built this cave?" Rae asked, opening one eye. "I suppose that means you are a smuggler too."

Samar shrugged. "Perhaps," he admitted. "Now, no more talking." Samar put the torch back into its holder at the cave's mouth. "This deep, noise does not travel easily, but I do not wish to take chances. Our lives may depend on it."

With that, he blew out the torch, leaving the cave in total darkness.

CHAPTER 13

It was raining in the desert. Pouring, actually, with large, cold drops falling on Jesse's face and jolting him out of a pleasant dream. Even before he opened his eyes, Jesse thought something must be wrong.

He blinked. Rae and Silas were leaning over him, trying not to laugh. A drop of water fell off of Silas' outstretched finger onto Jesse's nose, and he jerked his hand back guiltily.

Jesse was hardly awake enough to glare, but he gave his best effort anyway. "Good morning to you too." He wiped his face on his sleeve, hoping he hadn't left streaks of dirt and sand on his face.

"Well, it was about time for you to wake up," Rae said. "It's already almost noon."

Jesse blinked in surprise. The only light in the cave came from the torch, relit and in its holder. *I guess not much sunlight gets down here, no matter what time of day it is.*

Silas handed Jesse the water skin he had been holding, and Jesse gulped a mouthful gratefully.

"An old Da'armon trick," Samar said, his wrinkled face breaking into a grin. He sat near the entrance of the cave. "It was amusing to watch. You talked in your sleep, you know."

"Glad you were entertained," Jesse muttered.

"Come," Samar said, holding out a wooden bowl. "You must be hungry."

Slowly, Jesse reached out to grab his staff and stood, despite the protests of his aching muscles. He stretched, wincing. "Ugh," he groaned. "I feel like I slept on a rock."

Samar gave him a puzzled look. "It was a joke, Samar," Jesse explained. He took the bowl the old man offered him.

"Honey loaf and dried salmon," Samar said. "Food served at the greatest of desert celebrations."

Jesse took a bite of the bread. It was a bit stale, but very good. "Well, we're still alive," Jesse said. "That's enough for me to celebrate."

"The danger's not over yet," Silas said grimly. "The Rebellion will not give up easily."

"The Rebellion?" Rae questioned. She had begun to pace along the edge of the cave. Jesse got the idea that she did not like being in such tight quarters. She turned to Samar. "I thought you said it was Patrol members who were searching for us."

"Not all who wear the uniform are Patrol, Rae," Silas reminded her. "After all, why would the king's own men be trying to kill us? It makes no sense. Clearly, members of the Rebellion stole the uniforms as a disguise."

But Samar shook his head. "No," he said. "It cannot be. Even in the dark, I recognized one of the party who came

to meet me last night: Captain Demetri, the leader of the Patrol here. I am sure of it."

For a moment, Silas looked confused. Then he shook his head. "A traitor, perhaps. The Rebellion has been known to gain access to even high offices in the kingdom."

Slowly, Samar nodded in agreement. "It is possible," he conceded. "I've always known there was something different about this captain. He is young, but clever in a way that most Patrol members are not."

"Yes." Silas spat on the ground. "That's how they are, treacherous as vipers." He gestured to the pit viper, dead where Jesse had struck it the night before. "And I hope they all meet a similar end."

"Well," Jesse said, wiping his mouth and setting his bowl down, "not to interrupt such a pleasant discussion, but I want to know when we're getting out of here."

"Agreed," Rae said immediately. She looked ready to climb up the ladder that very second.

Samar shrugged. "We do not have provisions to stay here much longer. We will wait until nightfall, of course."

"I'm not sure that's wise," Silas said. "What if the men from the camp are waiting to ambush us?"

"Use your head, boy," Samar said impatiently. "If they suspected we were down here, they would have sent someone down while we were asleep. They clearly do not know about the pit."

"But won't they be able to find us once we rejoin your caravan?" Jesse pointed out.

Samar shook his head. "I told my chief servant to take the caravan ahead to an arranged meeting place in Da'armos. He has done this before and will not be followed."

"Smugglers," Silas muttered, shaking his head.

"Then you will take us to Da'armos?" Rae asked.

Samar leaned against the wall of the cave wearily. "I have little choice. By saving your lives, I made myself an outlaw in Amarias. Captain Demetri does not seem to be the kind to give up searching so easily. Da'armos is the only place I have to go now."

He paused. "Which reminds me…why would a powerful captain and his men be interested in three young people, barely more than children?"

Jesse and Rae both looked to Silas, who looked torn.

"Silas," Jesse said, "after all this, he deserves to know."

Silas nodded crisply. "You must know that Da'armos sends a rich payment of tribute to the king of Amarias each year," he began. Samar nodded. "This year, for reasons that we have yet to discover, the payment never came."

"Is that so?" Samar asked. "I had not heard." Silas looked impatient at being interrupted. "Please, continue."

"We have been sent to request this payment, and the obidhala, the Scorpion's Jewel, to give to the conqueror of Da'armos as tribute."

Samar's bushy eyebrows lifted slightly. "And how," he said, "do you plan to do that?"

Silas shrugged. "We come on the authority of King Selen. We will seek audience with the Sheik, explain that the tribute is past due, and order them to send it and the obidhala with us to Amarias."

"Which is exactly why the Sheik would send a message to this King Selen of yours by simply having you killed," Samar said.

Jesse smiled smugly at Silas and Rae. Rae rolled her eyes.

"Do you really think, since you say he has not sent this year's tribute, he is feeling any fear and respect toward Amarias?" Samar shook his head. "No. You would be wise to go back where you came from and tell the king to send an army if he wants his tribute."

"We can't do that," Rae insisted. "We must complete the mission."

"Yes, because you are in the Youth Guard, of course," Samar said, shaking his head. "A foolish Amarian tradition. Too many of the young and brave have died these long years."

Jesse stared at him. "You mean that you knew all along?"

"All this talk of a mission by three young people," Samar said with a shrug. "It could be nothing else. I am well aware of the Youth Guard. I have heard of a squad before, five years ago, in this very desert."

"Really?" *There must be a story here.* "Who were they? What were they supposed to accomplish?"

"It is not a happy tale, Jesse. I do not know who they were or what their mission was, but they did not complete it." Samar closed his eyes, as if to put the memory out of his mind. "They died in the desert before even reaching their destination. Slaughtered by a band of Da'armon soldiers."

Jesse winced. *We could be next.*

"Four young people who died too young," Samar said sadly. "No. The Youth Guard is blind foolishness."

Silas didn't seem bothered by Samar's words. "We need a plan," he said, turning to Rae and Jesse. "I, for one, am not willing to stumble through the gate of Da'ra with no idea of what we will do when we arrive."

"But we don't know where the Scorpion's Jewel is kept," Rae pointed out, "or how well it is guarded, or the layout of the palace. There is not much we can plan."

Samar grunted. "The way you talk, it sounds as if you are going to steal the sacred obidhala."

Silence for a moment. "Yes, that was the general plan," Rae admitted. "You said yourself there was no way for us to demand it from the Sheik."

Samar grinned. "Well, it is not as if I've never stolen anything in my life. Only I usually call it 'trading by other means.'"

Jesse frowned at this. His father had always been a man of strict honesty, and he had taught Jesse to be the same. *But this must be different*, Jesse told himself. *And, anyway, who am I to say anything?*

"You are right in saying we need to know more," Samar said to Rae. "Theft is a complicated business."

To Jesse's surprise, Silas spoke up. "Nothing good will come of it. Mark my words."

"There is no other way," Samar said with a shrug.

"There might be," Jesse said. "We could trick them into giving it to us, or threaten attack, or perhaps make a

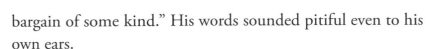

bargain of some kind." His words sounded pitiful even to his own ears.

"I was always taught that it was better to starve than steal," Silas explained, staring at Rae, as if his words were a challenge.

Rae sighed like Silas was a small child. "Times are hard, Silas, and sometimes that means we must take desperate measures. It may have been fine to hold on to those ideals at home when life was easy...."

"My life was never easy," Silas countered. "You know nothing of what I've been through. You know nothing of hardship."

Now it was Rae's turn to become angry. "And how do you know that? You think you're the only one who has suffered?"

Arguing again. Jesse wished he could disappear into the rock wall as the two glared at each other in the silence that followed.

"*Geriahiam den arameshin, den le'kavil,*" Samar said forcefully. They all stared at him. "Scars not worn with honor are worn for pity," he translated.

"I don't understand," Rae said flatly.

I do. Fumbling with the rough cloth, Jesse jerked up his pant leg to reveal his mangled left leg. Rae and Silas stopped glaring at each other to look. Jesse knew from their faces that they were repulsed by the sight.

Even though he knew it was ridiculous, at that moment, he felt like challenging Parvel's God. *My leg crippled. My parents gone without a trace. Silas' father dead. Parvel suffering from poison. Rae bitter and angry from some unknown pain. If You are there, why do You let it happen?*

He bit back the angry accusations and took a deep breath. "We all have scars," he said simply. "In the beginning, I called attention to my limp so people would feel sorry for me. But I soon learned that seeking pity was nothing but a crutch. Everyone suffers, and no one can say he has suffered more than another."

Silas and Rae just stared at him, but a quick glance at Samar told Jesse that his mind was on a different subject altogether. "A crutch…." he said, more to himself than the others. His face wrinkled in concentration. "Jesse, let me see that staff of yours."

Jesse handed it to him, and the old man stroked the intricate carvings. "Yes, it will be perfect," he replied, his eyes glinting with excitement. "There is very little wood in the desert. Only the rich and powerful own wooden items. Something this elaborate made out of wood will seem strange to them. It only needs one thing."

"What's that?" Jesse asked.

"The dead pit viper."

"Oh, no." Jesse grabbed the walking stick back. "That *thing* isn't coming anywhere near me or my staff."

"Calm yourself," Samar said impatiently. He gingerly picked up the dead viper and set it in Jesse's empty bowl, then wrapped it back in his pack. "We only need the viper to catch something else—the sacred creature of Da'armos."

This time Jesse was almost afraid to ask. "And what's that?"

"You've met one before. A kalthara."

"Oh, yes, the crazy vulture insect," Jesse said, wishing he hadn't asked. "The one that ate the scorpion that tried to kill me. Excellent idea, Samar."

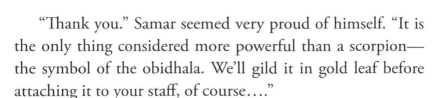

"Thank you." Samar seemed very proud of himself. "It is the only thing considered more powerful than a scorpion— the symbol of the obidhala. We'll gild it in gold leaf before attaching it to your staff, of course...."

"Wait," Jesse interrupted, holding his hand up. "Why? Why do all this?"

Samar grinned triumphantly. "You shall become, or at least they will think you are, a powerful sorcerer of the kaltharan cult!"

There was a pause. Then Rae and Silas burst out laughing.

"It is the only way for you to find out the location of the obidhala," Samar said, clearly not understanding their outburst. "I think the boy would make an excellent sorcerer."

They laughed harder. "Samariyosin, that is the most ridiculous thing I've ever heard," Rae gasped out.

"I am not finished yet," Samar said. His face was red with excitement. *Clearly, he doesn't care what Rae and Silas think of his plan.* "You," he pointed to Rae, "will also be in a disguise, as a common Da'armon woman."

Rae frowned. "Why me?"

"Because you have dark hair, of course." Samar stared at her carefully. "Your skin would give you away instantly, but I am, after all, a trader of spices and dyes. Surely we could find something to darken it."

"Wait," Silas said, shaking his head. "I still don't see what this has to do with acquiring the obidhala."

"You have admitted that you yourself know nothing of the obidhala," Samar pointed out. Silas nodded. "Then let me finish. I'll explain in good time." He stroked his thick beard in thought. "Of course, as the interpreter, I would need no disguise...."

"And where do I come into all this?" Silas interrupted.

Samar thought about that, then smiled. "Ah, I have it! You too will be disguised in a manner of speaking."

"As what?" Silas asked, still looking skeptical.

"The great sorcerer's slave, of course."

Jesse smiled. Samar was right. This would be a good plan.

CHAPTER 14

The streets of the capital city of Da'ra were crowded and noisy with people talking, laughing, shouting insults, haggling over prices, begging for money, calling out wares, and making themselves heard the same way they did every day.

But every voice stopped when Jesse limped past.

Jesse could only imagine how he looked. A young Amarian boy with a crippled leg, dressed in fine scarlet cloth with embroidery along the edges, carrying a staff with a kalthara on top, dipped in gold from Samar's caravan. He even had intricate designs of stars and moons painted on his forehead—Rae's idea.

"This is not going to work," Jesse muttered to Silas and Samar, who followed behind him, as all servants would near such a powerful person.

"Hold your head high," Samar whispered back. "Remember who you are supposed to be."

How does a sorcerer walk anyway? Jesse wondered. *Grandly, I suppose.* He made each step as confident as possible, never giving a glance at the Da'armons who stared and pointed at him.

One time, though, he risked a quick look to his left, just to make sure Rae was still there. That one glance was enough to make Jesse feel better. She moved with the crowd, her eyes downcast and her simple white garment making her blend in perfectly with the native Da'armons.

The streets between the clay-brick buildings were narrow and crowded, with clotheslines crossing the alleyways and vendors set up on every corner. Jesse should have had a difficult time getting through the crowd, but the people parted in front of him, stepping away from him and muttering. One mother held her child back, a frightened look on her face.

"Which way to the palace gate?" Jesse asked Samar, in a voice which he tried to make loud and booming. The last word was slightly choked off by the dust that billowed up from the street with every step.

"Straight ahead," Samar said. "Once we get there, do not say anything. I'll do the talking."

The whispers behind him became a jumbled babble, as more people crowded to see the strange boy and his servants. Jesse tried to ignore them, which is what he imagined a powerful sorcerer would do.

Because he was trying so hard to hold his head high, he nearly walked into a small, dead animal that lay in the street. Jesse couldn't tell what it was because it was covered with a swarm of hungry kaltharas. He shivered and decided to watch where he stepped.

"Jesse," Silas muttered. "Something isn't right. I say we turn back."

Jesse turned to look at him. Even dressed in rags, Silas was an imposing figure, making most of the Da'armons stay back. But he was glancing nervously around, as if expecting an attack on all sides.

It's because we wouldn't let him carry his bow, Jesse decided. *He feels vulnerable.* "We can't turn back now. It would be a waste of Rae's artwork on my forehead."

Silas was not amused. "We're being watched," he asserted. "I know it. I've felt it since we entered the city."

Before he could reply, Jesse saw something flying out of the corner of his eye and ducked. It was a rotten fruit of some kind.

The young man, who looked a few years older than Jesse, stepped out from the crowd. *"Na'halit les micre Amarian suler!"* he shouted. *"Alair de'haros!"*

Although Jesse could not understand him, he knew he was being mocked. *What would a sorcerer do?* Slowly, with measured steps and a perfectly calm expression on his face, Jesse walked toward the young man. He stretched out his hand toward him and separated his fingers one by one.

"You are as rotten as the fruit you threw," he muttered softly, looking the young man in the eye. "And twice as putrid smelling."

Ordinary words, but Jesse said them as if they were a magical curse of some kind. He continued to stare at the young man, who started to back away.

"Go home." Jesse's voice rose to a wail of doom. "Eat more of that fruit until you get sick to your stomach!"

From the confusion on his face, the young man clearly didn't understand Jesse's words, but Jesse's tone was plain enough. Confusion melted into fear, and the young man practically shoved his way through the crowd to get away from Jesse.

Jesse turned away and continued walking as if nothing had happened. Even over the crowd's mutters, he could hear Silas laughing quietly.

"Excellent performance," Samar whispered.

Jesse never looked back. "Thank you."

Soon the clay buildings and shabby carts of the main streets gave way to a thick wall, made of bricks dried solid from years of baking in the sun. *It must be wide enough for a horse to travel on top*, Jesse thought in awe.

Of course, he let none of his amazement show on his face. A powerful sorcerer would never be impressed by the palace of a mere mortal.

Two men armed with large spears stood at the gate in the wall. They stared straight ahead, pointed helmets pulled halfway over their faces and arms crossed. If he hadn't known better, Jesse would have thought they were statues.

"*Pedriamet*," Samar called in greeting.

As if it were some sort of signal, both men turned to face him. One of them barked out a question in Da'armon, to which Samar replied.

"They want to know what your business is here," Samar said to Jesse.

"Tell them that I must see the Sheik at once."

Samar relayed this message. Neither guard looked very happy. More questions followed, and Jesse tried to keep a look of haughty unconcern at all times as Samar answered for him. At one point, Samar slipped them a few silver coins. Still they did not move to open the gate.

"It is not good," Samar muttered to Jesse. "They say you are of the race of traitors and murderers. They ask you to prove your sorcery."

Jesse let his voice rise, as if he was offended by this request. "Silas," he said, "I'm going to need your help." True to his part as a servant, Silas did not protest.

I hope this works. Jesse turned again to Samar. "Tell the guards that I will show them the extent of my powers by inflicting a curse on my servant."

For a brief second, Samar gave Jesse a look of panic, as if to say, "Are you sure this is what you want to do?" Then, sighing slightly as if he did not believe Jesse himself, he rattled off a string of Da'armon to the guards, who began to laugh.

Ignoring them, Jesse fixed his eyes on Silas. He looked nervous, and Jesse was not sure if that was part of the act or not.

"I curse thee with terrible intestinal pain," Jesse chanted solemnly, walking around Silas in a circle. "It will make you wish you had never been born!" He slammed his staff down on the ground with the last word.

Instantly, Silas fell to the ground, screaming and clutching his stomach as if he were in intense pain. He clawed the dirt and writhed in agony, thrashing violently. Jesse had to keep himself from staring in amazement.

I almost feel like I really have put a curse on him, he marveled. Outwardly, he looked down coldly on his servant's display of pain.

Already a crowd of alarmed Da'armons had gathered. One woman was wailing, as if begging Jesse to stop. He let Silas scream a while longer, then shouted, "Enough," banging the staff against the ground again.

Silas stopped, breathing heavily. Slowly, he stood, looking disoriented, and dusted himself off. The noise of the crowd died to an awed murmur.

"If you do not let us in, you will be next," Jesse declared, pointing at the guards with his staff. Even if they did not understand his words, they could not miss his message.

The fear on their faces nearly made Jesse want to dance right there in the street. "*Harlid mahat!*" one of the guards called.

The gate began to lift.

"That," Jesse said quietly as they paraded through the gates, "was probably the most impressive display I've ever seen. If you survive the Youth Guard, you should join a traveling theatre troupe, Silas."

"If I survive," Silas reminded him. "Let's focus on that right now."

At least, Jesse thought, *Rae made it through*. Her familiar face was among the throng of Da'armons who had pushed through the gate, despite the weak protests of the guards. If the mob wanted a show, they would have it.

Samar, at least, was confident they would succeed. If the clothes, painted designs, and staff were not enough, Samar had insisted that Jesse's limp would be a key detail in his favor. "Da'armos is a harsh land," he said. "Not many who have deformities survive for long. Those who do are considered marked by fate for greatness. Local folk tales tell of heroes who had to be wounded by the gods so they would not be able to overthrow them. That is what they will remember when they see you."

For the first time since the accident, then, Jesse's crippled leg was proving to be an advantage. *I hope it's enough of an advantage,* he thought, as the guards flung open the gates of the palace, the central building in the courtyard.

Once again, Jesse had to bite his tongue to keep from gasping as he entered the palace hall. *Incredible.* The walls were hung with woven straw mats that featured brightly painted scenes, stretching from floor to ceiling, and the windows were framed with designs in gold.

And, at the front of the room, a man sat on an enormous wooden throne. He was dressed in purple robes and a turban adorned with the largest emerald Jesse had ever seen. Five servants with reed fans kept a constant cooling breeze on his face.

"This Sheik has only been ruling for two years," Samar whispered to Jesse. "That is, perhaps, good for us. He is young and inexperienced."

The Sheik stared at the new arrivals with a bored, arrogant grimace on his face. Jesse judged him to be cocky, more concerned with impressing than ruling.

"You'll have more trouble with the *ha'lit*, Benotan," Samar said, indicating an older man standing to the right of the throne. "He has served three generations of Sheiks." The man was staring at Jesse with suspicion, paying no notice to the crowd of commoners.

"The Sheik looks like a peacock I once saw in a minstrel show," Jesse said to Samar and Silas—a little too loudly.

Briefly, Jesse saw the one Samar called Benotan turn toward him. He might have imagined it, because it was gone the next instant, but Jesse was almost sure he saw a smile on the man's face. *He understands me*, Jesse realized. It was an important thing to know. This time, he must choose his words carefully.

"*Pedriamet*," Samar called, bowing to the ground. Silas bowed too, and made a motion for Jesse to do the same. He did not.

I'm going to get his attention eventually anyway, Jesse decided, never looking away from the young ruler.

The Sheik didn't appear to notice. He sighed and asked Samar a question in Da'armon.

More formalities. Jesse sighed. It was stiflingly hot in the hall, and he hated not being able to understand what anyone was saying. *A powerful sorcerer doesn't have to wait for anyone, even a Sheik.*

He slammed down his staff, cutting Samar off in the middle of a sentence. "Hear me well, all you people," he declared with as much authority as he could find within himself. "I have traveled far and seen many rulers."

He barely waited for Samar to finish translating before he continued. "I have been given divine wisdom to discern which rulers are cruel and greedy. Many are, and they must pay the price. We shall soon see if the ruler of your land is among them."

Benotan frowned and started to speak, but Jesse cut him off. "Those whose leaders rule with a fist of iron and a heart of stone will have their greatest treasure, the source of their power, turned into iron and stone."

As Samar relayed his message, Jesse heard a new word spread through the crowd, "obidhala."

Feeling rather ridiculous, he began dancing in a circle in front of the throne, chanting nonsense words and lifting his staff into the air. *Rae must be enjoying this.*

With a final pound from his staff, Jesse stopped, eyes frozen on the Sheik, who looked slightly confused. Jesse turned instead to the advisor, Benotan. "Bring out the obidhala," Jesse commanded. "We will see what the leader of your land is truly like."

Benotan did not even wait for Samar to finish translating. "You think we must listen to your demands?" he scoffed.

Jesse had been ready for this, of course. "The only way to get him to bring out the obidhala," Samar had told him earlier, "is to manipulate him through the people."

"I see that you're afraid." Jesse said, walking closer to the advisor.

"Keep your distance, Amarian," he snapped, edging away as if Jesse had some sort of rare disease.

"You're afraid of what will happen when the people find out that your obidhala is nothing but a block of stone. You're afraid of losing power."

More mutters from the crowd as Samar translated his bold words. Jesse almost expected another piece of rotten fruit to come flying through the air.

Another step forward. This time, Jesse lowered his voice, so that only Benotan could hear. "And power is the only reason you rule, isn't it?" The expression of hatred on his face was answer enough, and Jesse nodded with satisfaction. "Then my curse was well-placed. You do have reason to fear."

"You go too far, boy," Benotan hissed.

Jesse shrugged casually. "I merely state what the people will think. If you refuse to show them the obidhala, they will assume that it did turn to stone. Perhaps it will be enough to remind them of the evil of their leaders. You are heavily outnumbered. An uprising of any strength would succeed."

Although Jesse's logic was sound, Benotan still hesitated. *He can't actually believe that I have the power to curse the obidhala...can he?*

Restless, some in the crowd began to mutter, until one man raised a shout. It was soon echoed by others, "*Padrok le'obidhala!*"

His face expressionless, Samar turned to Jesse and the Sheik. "They ask that the obidhala be brought out and presented to them."

The Sheik seemed to consider this, although he still looked confused. Jesse held his breath as Benotan whispered something in his ear.

The Sheik nodded, then made a proclamation in Da'armon that made the people cheer. "For my people, I will do this,"

Samar translated. "I shall not be made a mockery by this Amarian pretender."

He clapped his hands, and the two guards at the hall door crossed over to a door near the throne room. *They are going to the storehouse where the treasures are kept,* Jesse guessed.

If Jesse had not been watching carefully, he would not have noticed Rae following. She moved lightly along the back of the room, carrying a basket of grain, as if she were on her way to the kitchen. No one would take any notice of her. She was perfect in her role.

It was true with all of them, Jesse realized. They each had their own strengths that contributed to the success of the mission, and they had already saved each others' lives many times. Parvel had been right—they could not have done this alone. They needed each other.

Everyone else was staring at him, and Jesse felt oddly like a juggler who, once onstage, has no act to perform. He settled for crossing his arms and trying to look intimidating. *All I can do is wait.*

Samar's plan had been simple. Rae must find out where the obidhala was kept, take note of its surroundings, and report back to them. It was a classic trick used by pickpockets: force the victim to unknowingly reveal the hiding place of a valuable.

Once the people saw that the obidhala had not turned to stone, Jesse would be jeered at and laughed out of the palace, but they would have the information they needed to decide what to do next.

The plan did not involve someone bursting into the throne room, shouting in Da'armon.

Jesse turned around to see a man standing in the doorway, wearing the dark blue uniform of the Patrol with the black cape of a captain. His skin was dark, and his square jaw was stiff in a scowl. The two guards stood behind him, although they were partially blocked from view by the captain's large frame.

"Demetri," Samar muttered. His voice sounded slightly panicked.

For a moment, the man just stood there, breathing hard. He glanced at Jesse, then Silas, and nodded, a look of triumph on his face.

Then he grabbed someone from behind the guards and pulled her into the room.

Jesse froze. It was Rae, her white headdress ripped aside and her eyes defiant.

The captain held her wrist high into the air and shouted something in Da'armon. Then he looked straight at Jesse. "This girl is with the sorcerer! She tried to steal the obidhala!"

Shouts of outrage were already erupting from the crowd. This time, at least the Sheik had an easy decision to make. He shook his fist at his remaining guards and called out an order.

The captain, Demetri, never looked away from Jesse. The man was smiling—*smiling!*—as he roughly shoved Rae to the guard in the doorway. "Take them to the dungeons. By order of the Sheik."

CHAPTER 15

After five hours in his dungeon cell, Jesse had memorized every detail of it: every brick, every crack, every stain.

Not that there was much to memorize. The cell would take four steps to cross in any direction. Of course, Jesse was not permitted to cross the cell. He was chained firmly to the wall by his hands and his ankles. The guard who had locked the chains had enjoyed laughing at Jesse's crippled left leg, even kicking it once. Jesse had responded by muttering a fake curse at him. The guard left him alone after that.

Near the wall where he was chained was a pot of dirty water that he assumed was used for drinking. There were two locks on the door, one near the top and another near the floor. A scorpion, dead for an indefinite amount of time, lay in the corner.

That's one good thing about a dungeon with no windows, Jesse thought. *None of those horrible katharas can reach it here.*

They had taken the golden kalthara off of his staff. *Some jailer will probably give the trinket to his wife tonight,* thought wryly. He had been allowed to keep the walk stick. From the looks on the guards' faces, he assumed this was because of his reputation for sorcery. *But what good will my walking stick do when I'm chained in a dungeon?*

A rattling of keys down the hallway told Jesse the hourly inspection had come again. That was how he was able to keep time in the prison. Each hour, a guard would check to make sure he was still there, still chained, and still miserable.

Sure enough, a figure in black came into view through the thick steel bars of the cell. The prison guards, as far as Jesse could tell, were the only Da'armons forced to wear dark clothing in the desert heat. *Maybe that's why they all seem to be so ill-tempered.*

This one was no different. He unlocked the door to the cell, muttering under his breath, probably about all the trouble he had to go to for a foreigner.

Then he stepped closer. *Interesting. The others acted as if they were trained to keep their distance, in case a prisoner got close enough to somehow steal their weapon.*

Of course, Jesse had no such plans. He could hardly move his arms away from the brick wall.

The guard looked behind him quickly, then took another step toward Jesse. "I have a message for you," the guard said, in heavily accented Amarian. "From the one who has no fear."

Samar. Jesse concentrated on every word the guard spoke, knowing it would not be repeated.

"He says, 'I have friends in high places. Fear not the vultures. Run to me when the time is right.'"

"That's all?"

But the guard was already stomping away, making a show of locking the door loudly and deliberately. He marched back down the hall, leaving Jesse alone with his thoughts. *Samar must have a plan to get us out of here. But what?* Jesse thought again of the words of the message. *'Friends in high places.' That must be the guard. But what vultures? And how will I know when the time is right?*

Those questions, at least for the moment, had no answer, so Jesse pushed them away. He also refused to think of his parents, or Parvel, or Parvel's God, or what would happen to him, or a thousand other unpleasant subjects that crowded his mind, demanding attention. He just stood in silence and stared at the wall like he had for hours on end.

Once, he had heard a traveler at the inn tell of the prison at Terenid, the capital of Amarias. The huge stone tower was crammed with people, all sleeping on the same rancid straw, fighting each other for the scraps of food that would be thrown to them every now and then.

This was altogether different. Jesse knew there would be no one to talk to or argue with, no one to discuss what might happen next, no one to help him if he got sick or cry for him if he was taken away to be executed. *The Da'armons must understand the power of loneliness far better than we Amarians do.*

Just when Jesse had realized he needed Rae and Silas, they were taken away from him. *If you are there, God, if you really do exist, then show yourself! Do something!* He threw the prayer up to the brick ceiling like he would throw a stone at a vicious dog.

There was no answer.

Time seemed to crawl by, so Jesse was surprised to hear more footsteps in the dungeon hall. *Surely another hour couldn't have passed already.*

This time, though, there were three men: two guards, and the captain who had caught Rae, the one Samar had called Captain Demetri. Jesse refused to look at him and studied the floor instead.

"*Yasim'et*," Captain Demetri ordered. "Leave us."

The guards did not seem to appreciate this order, and they argued with the captain for a while. After a few harsh words, the captain seemed to have won, because Jesse heard two pairs of retreating footsteps.

Neither Jesse nor Captain Demetri said a word. Finally, Jesse couldn't stand it any longer. He lifted his head to face the man.

Apparently that was enough of a show of weakness for Captain Demetri to speak. "They say you have no Guard tattoo on your shoulder," he said.

Jesse said nothing.

"Tell me," Captain Demetri said, "why were there only two Guard members in your party?"

Again, Jesse said nothing.

"The other two told their stories. I must see if your answer matches," Captain Demetri said in a weary tone.

That surprised Jesse, and it must have shown on his face, because Captain Demetri explained, "Each one was most helpful when I threatened to kill the other two members of the group. You will do the same. If you do not give us this

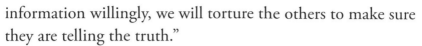

information willingly, we will torture the others to make sure they are telling the truth."

"One member of the squad died in training," Jesse said flatly. "Another is sick with poison back at the village of Mir."

"Very good," Captain Demetri said, apparently satisfied. "I don't know how you got mixed in with those two, but my orders were for them and any with them."

"What orders?" Jesse demanded.

Captain Demetri ignored him. "Your friend, the translator, will go free. He is partly of the Da'armon people and claims that he knew nothing of your scheme."

"What orders?"

"Kill the Youth Guard members who came through my town," the captain said bluntly. "And that is what will happen. Even if I had not been here, you would have been executed by the Sheik for your pathetic attempt at theft."

Jesse studied Captain Demetri's Patrol uniform. It looked genuine, not like a homemade copy.

"Where did you steal the Patrol uniform?" Jesse asked bitterly. "It's an excellent disguise for a member of the Rebellion."

The captain laughed, a deep laugh that somehow seemed familiar. "Is that what you think?"

Jesse blinked, caught off-guard by the sudden laughter. "I don't understand…."

"No, you don't. Of course you don't." Captain Demetri said softly. He got a far-off look on his face. "They don't want you to. Even I didn't understand at first."

"What do you mean?"

Captain Demetri smiled slightly, and Jesse got the feeling that he enjoyed tormenting him. "All I will say is this: I have learned that you must be careful who your friends are. They may well be your enemies."

There was silence for a moment as Jesse thought about what Captain Demetri had said. *What does he mean? That the king is our enemy?* "No," Jesse said, with more conviction than he felt. "You're lying. Silas said all those in the Rebellion lie."

"That may be," Captain Demetri said with a shrug. "But if it is, it is because everyone lies. Do you hear me, boy? Everyone. Remember that."

"Why are you telling me all this?"

A grim smile from the captain. "It is a good question. You will not live long enough to learn these lessons, true though they are. The Sheik has ordered that the three of you be given the death penalty for your crime."

Though the cell was still boiling hot, Jesse felt a chill go through him. Captain Demetri turned to go. "Wait," Jesse said, deciding to take a guess at what Captain Demetri meant. "Why does the king want to kill us?"

Captain Demetri answered his question with a question. "Why do you want to know?"

Jesse shrugged, tried to act calm. "Curiosity." When the captain still hesitated, he added, "You said yourself that there is no way for us to avoid our death in the morning. What harm could it do to explain to me why we are dying?"

"True enough," Captain Demetri acknowledged. "All

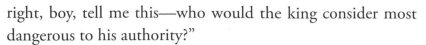

right, boy, tell me this—who would the king consider most dangerous to his authority?"

"The leaders of the Rebellion," Jesse replied immediately, "or spies from other countries."

"Yes," Captain Demetri agreed, "but those are easy enough to deal with. If the Patrol even suspects citizens of being Rebellion members, they can execute them without a trial. Any charge will do. The difficulty is preventing people from joining the Rebellion in the first place."

Jesse thought about that. *It is true, I suppose.* "But what does that have to do with us?"

"What is the function of the Youth Guard?"

Jesse repeated the answer he had heard since he was a young boy, "To accomplish great missions for the king."

"Then why aren't they given enough information to succeed at these missions?" Captain Demetri asked, his voice emotionless. "Why do so few survive, out of the hundreds who have gone out?" They were good questions, ones that Jesse had often asked himself.

"If King Selen had wanted an army," the captain continued, "those skilled in agility, strength, and battle tactics, he would have chosen his top Patrol members for these missions. But he wanted something more—the most intelligent, the most dedicated young people in the country. Why?"

Captain Demetri answered his own question, "Because those are the ones who, if they decided to take action, would be the most powerful force against him. He is afraid of your friends and those like them."

The truth of it became clear to Jesse. All these years, he had thought the reason so few Youth Guard members ever returned was because of the danger of their missions. But now he knew: they did not return because the king did not want them to return.

He had always known the king was a greedy, self-serving man, taking half of their crops and many of their young men and women to use as his slaves, feasting while his people starved. It was one thing to cheat a nation of faceless peasants out of their living. But it was quite another to deliberately kill innocent young people, just to eliminate a potential threat.

"And so the king sends people like you to kill us," Jesse summarized, disgust plain in his voice.

The captain's hand went up to his chest, and he clutched something underneath his uniform. Then he shrugged. "*Oldrivar lakita ses omidreden.* Your friends must be prepared to reap the whirlwind that they released. They knew what they were doing when they agreed to join the Youth Guard. And, besides, I had very little choice. Someone else's life depends on my obedience."

"But that's not right!"

Captain Demetri stepped forward slightly, scowling at Jesse. "Life is not right sometimes, boy. I've had to learn that the hard way." He began to march away, then turned. "And this time, life has decided that you will die."

CHAPTER 16

Dawn always comes too soon, Jesse decided as the guard unlocked his chains from the wall of the dungeon. He wished for the days when he would wake at the inn in Mir, grumbling before going to do his chores. Now there was a much more serious reason for him to dread the dawn.

The guard shoved him out of the cell, shouting at him in Da'armon. "Lead the way," Jesse said, as cheerfully as he could, even though he knew the guard would not understand his words. "Beautiful morning, isn't it?"

The look on the guard's face was reward enough for the attempt at a joke. Clearly, he was not used to such a compliant prisoner, much less one with light skin, the carved walking stick of a sorcerer, and strange markings on his forehead.

Still, Jesse's cheerfulness wasn't entirely forced. Samar's message gave him a little hope. Enough, at least, to allow him to hold his head up as the guard marched him through the dungeon.

The guard yelled something in Da'armon and reached for Jesse's walking stick, which he jerked back, giving the guard a cold glare. It was awkward, of course, to hold onto the walking stick while he was chained, but Jesse would not leave it in the Da'armon dungeon.

His one comfort was being reunited with Rae and Silas. Both looked dirty and tired, although Rae was the most disheveled by far, with sweat creating smudges in the dye that covered her face.

"Are you all right?" Jesse asked them.

One of the guards shouted at him in Da'armon and gave him a sharp poke with his spear, to make sure Jesse understood. Jesse saw a small pool of blood form from the pierced skin. *I guess that means no more talking.*

He remained silent. The only sound came from the clinking of the chains around their ankles as they were marched through the prison gates and out into the streets of Da'ra. Then the silence stopped.

A human whirlwind—that's what the throngs of people outside the gates reminded Jesse of, all moving, convulsing, swirling around him and never stopping—like the sand that had buried them in the desert. The people thronged toward them, held back only by threats from the guards. After that they seemed content to jeer at a distance, calling out insults Jesse was glad he couldn't understand. *It seems like we can't go anywhere in this country without being surrounded by a noisy crowd.*

Although Jesse searched the crowd as well as he could with the guards prodding him to go faster, he did not see Samar's face. *He must be here. He must.*

Soon, the execution site came into view.

Jesse knew it was the execution site—it could be nothing else. Three pyres of wood were stacked on a platform made of clay bricks. The platform was built against the palace wall, and the Sheik sat on his throne nearby, with Benotan beside him.

Although the Sheik looked half-asleep, his turban jammed down on his face to cover his ears from the noise of the crowd, it seemed to Jesse that Benotan was drilling him with a haughty stare that said, "We defeated you, Sorcerer." Jesse nodded politely at him and smiled to himself when Benotan's confident expression faltered. *Not yet.*

Beside him, Rae gasped and stepped backward, nearly falling into him. Jesse peered over her shoulder trying to see....

He blinked, making sure his eyes had not deceived him. The wall of the palace was moving! A second glance told Jesse why. Clinging to the wall, were hundreds—perhaps thousands—of kaltharas. The bricks quivered with them, and the air hummed with their high-pitched scream, an undercurrent beneath the cries of the people.

Fear not the vultures. Samar's message began to make sense. The kaltharas also knew the platform was an execution site. They were waiting for the Youth Guard members. Waiting for them to die.

Suddenly, Jesse was not quite so confident. Looking at the scavengers who would fight over his dead body, escape seemed impossible. The guards never looked away from them, and they were tightly chained. As if that weren't enough, hundreds of Da'armons had come to watch the execution. *Even if Samar is here, what could he possibly do?*

Playing games with death. If, as Parvel had said, this was a game, it was being watched by an eager crowd of spectators— some jeering angrily, but most looking excited, as if it were a festival of some sort.

So this is it. He and Rae and Silas were going to die. Jesse could do nothing to save himself. *Why is Parvel always right?* he thought bitterly.

The guards shoved them in front of the platform with the pyres. Jesse nearly tripped over his chains and fell into Silas. Behind him, the hum of the kaltharas seemed to mock him and his hopes.

God, if you're there at all, and if you're listening, rescue us! It was the only prayer Jesse could think of. He was sure the village priest would not approve.

A Da'armon official stepped in front of them, reading from a parchment of some sort. *Animal skin*, Jesse thought, *because wood is rare here.* He thought about that, almost in a detached way, as if he wasn't about to die. *Then why choose burning for an execution?* He decided they must be very important prisoners, a fact that did little to cheer him.

While the official babbled on, Jesse scanned the crowd again, looking for a familiar face.

There! Relief flooded Jesse like a bucket of cool water poured over his head. Off to the side, standing against the palace wall, was Samar. He glanced at Jesse briefly, nodded, and pulled a hood over his face.

He glanced at Silas and Rae to see if they had seen him too. Rae, at least, had, because her eyes were fixed on that part of the wall. "Be ready," he whispered to them, hoping the

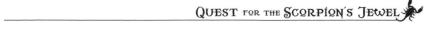

guards would not overhear and poke him again. Silas and Rae nodded slightly.

I could probably deliver a dramatic speech and no one would hear over the voices of the crowd, Jesse realized. They only occasionally quieted down to hear the man with the parchment speak. No doubt they had heard the same words before, and wanted to get on with the execution.

The drone of the kaltharas could be heard in the rare quiet moments. Jesse saw Rae's head jerk toward the wall every now and then. Each time, she would shiver and shrink just a little closer toward Silas and Jesse.

"It will be all right," Silas said. Although his words were confident, his face was not.

Jesse was only slightly more hopeful. *If Samar is going to do something at all,* he decided, *it would have to be when they take off our chains to tie us to the pyres.* After all, they could not climb up onto the platform with their ankles bound.

He glanced toward Samar again. He took off his hood, as if to say, "Get ready."

Jesse looked around. Four guards surrounded them, and two more stood beside the king. All of them were large, strong men with spears at the ready. Their chances were not good, he knew.

But I'd rather die trying to escape, Jesse decided. A quick glance at the other two told him that they felt the same. Silas stood straight and tall, his steely gray eyes betraying no emotion at all. Rae defied the crowd with her haughty stare, refusing to let their taunts shame her.

They are braver than I am. Jesse's legs felt weak underneath him, and he began to feel dizzy. *Focus,* he commanded himself. *You have to be ready.*

On some signal from the official, three of the guards began to unlock their chains, first from around their wrists, then their ankles. While the guards stooped to the ground, Jesse kept his eyes fixed on Samar, watching, waiting.

The chains had barely fallen to the ground when someone in the crowd screamed. Jesse jerked his eyes toward the sound and saw the Sheik's throne licked with flames. A flaming arrow, a second one, whistled through the air and hit the platform behind him. Then three more at once, all from different directions, hit the pyres of wood, and they burst into flames.

The guards around the Sheik were frantically trying to put out the fire. One threw the Sheik to the ground, trying to douse the flames that had caught onto his robes. The guards around Jesse didn't seem to know what to do.

In that instant, Jesse looked over at Samar. He nodded. *Run to me when the time is right.*

Jesse turned to shout a signal to Rae and Silas, but, for a moment, no words would come.

For, in that moment, figures appeared from the top of the palace wall and emptied huge cauldrons of water downward.

And the wall of kaltharas exploded.

Everyone in the crowd seemed frozen. "Run!" Jesse shouted, and that one word seemed to turn the streets into a stampede as the dark cloud of insects swooped toward them.

Vaguely he saw Rae and Silas on either side of him. Rae was holding Silas' hand, her eyes squeezed shut, sobbing and

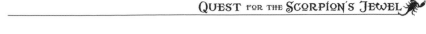

batting the kaltharas away as best she could.

Then Samar's face, framed by the gray hood, appeared in front of them. "Follow me!" he called.

Jesse could do nothing else. Without someone to follow, somewhere to go, he would have been like anyone else in the crowd: panicked and disoriented. People ran and fell and shouted around him, not appearing to notice the escaping prisoners.

Above it all was the high-pitched wail of the kaltharas, so loud that Jesse felt his eardrums would burst. It was all he could do to keep from dropping to the ground and covering his head with his hands. Anything, anything to block out the noise.

Instead, he shoved people aside with his walking stick, trying to keep pace with Samar. At any second, he expected to feel a spear in his back. But the spear never came.

The smoke cleared after they had run a few streets, and the kaltharas were fewer. Jesse flicked a kalthara off of his shoulder. They were falling now, their agonized panic lessening as the effects of the water wore off. *Our cover will soon be gone,* Jesse thought. He glanced down at his ridiculous costume. *And I, at least, cannot hide.*

As if hearing his thoughts, a voice from behind him shouted, "After them! Don't let the prisoners escape!"

Jesse didn't need to turn around to know who it was. The man had spoken in Amarian. *Captain Demetri.*

"Do not stop!" Samar yelled, as if they might have considered it. He began darting through alleys now, avoiding gutters and ducking under lines of laundry strung out to dry.

Jesse was falling behind. His left leg began to ache dully, and his breathing was heavier. Samar ducked down passages so quickly that Jesse could hardly see where he had gone. "Come on, Jesse!" Rae called, glancing back at him.

The others slowed down, waiting for him to catch up. Behind them, Captain Demetri's voice was louder, still trying to rally someone to his aid. As far as Jesse could tell, he was their only pursuer. They could not lose him; he was too fast.

If I stay with them, they'll all be caught, Jesse realized. *I'm slowing them down.*

Jesse made his decision. Even though it went against everything his panicked mind was screaming at him, he stopped and turned around, slowly and deliberately. The others kept running. *With any luck, they'll already be away before they realize I'm gone.*

Jesse didn't move as Captain Demetri ran down the alley toward him. He paused a few steps before reaching Jesse, clearly expecting a trap. "Where did they go?" he demanded. "Tell me, and I will spare your life."

Jesse didn't answer.

"They will be caught, no matter what you do," Captain Demetri said, taking a step closer, his sword raised. "The Da'armons have already closed every gate of the city. Ten guards are stationed at each, searching everyone who leaves. The other guards will search door to door, every house and attic and cellar. They will find your friends, and they will kill them."

Jesse never backed down. "Then they'll have to do it on their own. I will not betray the members of my squad."

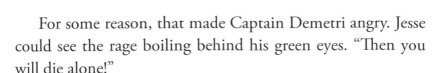

For some reason, that made Captain Demetri angry. Jesse could see the rage boiling behind his green eyes. "Then you will die alone!"

Jesse ducked as Captain Demetri thrust his sword forward, scrambling back on the dusty street. *He won't miss again*, he thought desperately.

Then, movement to his left. The sound of metal against metal.

Jesse looked up. It was Silas, a short broadsword locked with Captain Demetri's. "You!" Captain Demetri exclaimed. He recovered quickly, his darting eyes making sure Silas was alone. "So you hope to best a Patrol captain at swordplay, young Guard member?"

"No," Silas said, calmly meeting his gaze. He simply stepped aside.

With a blood-chilling cry, Rae jumped from the roof of the building. She grabbed onto a clothesline and launched herself, feet first, at Captain Demetri's chest.

He collapsed, his head hitting a stone doorstep with a sickening thud. Blood oozed from his temple and soaked into the dust. He did not move.

Silas raised his sword to stab the fallen captain. "Don't!" Jesse blurted, without realizing why. "He can't even fight back."

"He tried to kill you," Silas pointed out.

"Leave him," Rae said, letting go of the clothesline and landing lightly on her feet. "There's no time to argue."

They turned the corner, where Samar was standing, looking anxious. His face brightened as soon as he saw them.

"I will have my sword back, if you please," he said to Silas.

"I thought you told us to leave our weapons at the camp so we wouldn't raise suspicions," Jesse said.

"Did I tell *myself* to leave the weapons at the camp?" Samar replied. He returned the sword to a sheath strapped to his back.

Rae glanced back. "Let's get away from here before someone finds the captain, or us."

They began to run again. "Not much farther now," Samar called. They rejoined the throng of people on the main street, still babbling in confusion.

"Come," Samar shouted, waving them over toward the city wall. It was even thicker than the wall of the palace and studded with large metal spikes.

After giving a quick glance around, Samar knelt by the city wall and pulled a metal grate from the ground. "Drop down," he ordered, disappearing into the hole beneath the grate.

Jesse followed, although his nose and his stomach told him not to. *What a horrible stench!*

The hole led to what seemed to be a shallow pit, small and filled with sewage that Jesse was glad it was too dark to identify. He willed himself not to look, not to breathe, as he followed Samar through the tunnel. At one point, he was forced to stoop almost to his knees. *How will Silas fit?* From the grunts behind him, he could tell it was a difficult task.

Finally, the ground beneath him became firm. Still, Samar did not slow his pace, ducking and crawling through a tunnel that seemed to wind aimlessly through the desert.

Jesse tripped over one of the bricks that lined the tunnel on all sides. This time, he could not find the strength to stand again. "Samar," Jesse gasped, "we must rest."

Samar stopped, and Jesse was surprised to hear that he was barely breathing hard. "Perhaps it is safe to wait here for a while," he agreed.

Silas and Rae collapsed behind him, and Jesse felt better, listening to their gasps of exhaustion. Though they were younger than Samar, they were weakened from a day in the prison without food. *And I imagine Samar has used this route to escape before.*

For a moment, Jesse just lay there, trying to breathe and trying to stop his heart from exploding in his chest. The smell of sewage was strong, and Jesse knew they must be covered in it. At the moment, he did not care. *At least we're alive.*

Silas was the first one to speak. "Where are we?" he asked.

"You are in the sewer under the city gates," Samar responded. "The West Side is home to the butchers of Da'armos. It is the most unlikely sewer to be searched, especially on a hot spring day. We are safe here."

Slowly realizing what he had been wading through, Jesse felt sick. Since he had been given no food in the prison, he merely moaned, trying to control his nauseous stomach.

"Of course, this system of tunnels could not be found in any of the other sewers," Samar continued, as if he didn't realize the effect of his last statement. "It was built, again, by smugglers. There are many of them in Da'armos, maybe even more than in your country. This is one of their secret places around the city of Da'ra."

"The kaltharas," Rae said, her voice sounding small and empty of her usual confidence. "They came from everywhere."

"Again, smugglers," Samar said. "After you were taken away, I did not know what to do. I wandered around the streets for a while, but no answer came to me. Finally, for the first time in my life, I prayed."

At that, Rae groaned out loud. Samar seemed to ignore this outburst and continued, "I said, 'O God, if the One who numbers the stars cares about the lives of men, give me a way to save my friends.'"

His prayer was much more eloquent than mine.

"And then I, quite literally, ran into my old friend Ha'latem. I was praying with my eyes closed, you see," Samar explained, "and didn't notice Ha'latem's fish cart. He's the wiliest merchant you'll ever meet. Escaped from the Da'armon dungeon nothing short of five times. He was the one who came up with the plan."

"Which was…." Silas prompted, when it appeared Samar was not planning to continue.

"You might have seen the figures on the wall pouring the water and shooting the flaming arrows?" Jesse nodded. "Friends of mine who owed me many favors. We smugglers may be as dishonest as thieves, but we're very loyal. And," he added, "none of them have great love for the Sheik."

Friends in high places. The palace wall was indeed a high place.

"Once you are rested, we will continue on," Samar said. "The tunnel leads outside of the city. From there we will go to a small oasis known for its bitter water. They will not search for us there."

Jesse was content just to stay there for the moment, sewage or not. It felt good to be free of the chains around his ankles. To hear nothing but the heavy breathing of his friends. To smell.... *Well, maybe fresh air would be nice. But it can wait.*

In the dark, Samar began to chuckle softly.

"What is it?" Jesse asked.

"Do you realize how this will appear?" Samar asked. *Jesse felt too tired to think of an answer. Samar gave his own.* "On the day the kaltharan sorcerer was to be executed, he smote the city with a cloud of kaltharas and fire, and disappeared!"

Now Jesse began to laugh too, remembering the panic and confusion they had created.

"Mark my words, Jesse," Samar said. "Da'armons will tell their children stories about this day for centuries to come."

Well, I guess I became a legend after all. It was not exactly the way Jesse had imagined it. *But it will have to do. Maybe the Da'armons will even name a star after me.*

CHAPTER 17

When Jesse awoke the next afternoon, he felt more tired than he had before he fell asleep. His shirt stuck to his sweaty skin—even the light cloth of the tent seemed to trap the desert heat. He was thirsty and his body was still sore, but there was something more than that. *Something's wrong. But what?*

Everything seemed to be fine. They had left the city undetected and traveled all night to get to the oasis. There, they had eaten and then slept all through the morning, if the sun's position in the sky were any clue. There had been no alarms, no assassins, no sign of trouble at all.

Jesse found Silas and Rae crouched beside the firepit, eating something out of a bowl. They looked clean, rested, and at ease. *That's because nothing is wrong*, Jesse told himself. *We're safe now.*

Jesse sat down beside them, trying to make himself comfortable in the sand. It felt strange, moving in the open without hiding, but Samar had assured them he had guards posted in a wide circle around the camp, ready to alert them at the slightest hint of danger.

"Here," Rae said, handing him a bowl. "Breakfast."

Jesse made a face at the small, wrinkled shapes in the bowl. He poked one. It was sticky and leathery. *Kaltharas?*

"Don't be a coward," Rae said, as if reading his mind. "It's just dried fruit."

"I knew that." He popped a few in his mouth and chewed. Tough, but sweet.

"Did you sleep well?" Silas asked.

"Well enough," Jesse lied.

"You talked in your sleep again," Silas said mildly.

"Shouted, actually," Rae said. "Like someone was attacking you. I heard you from the other tent and made Silas check on you. You must have been having a nightmare."

"Maybe," Jesse said. Something nagged at the back of his mind, something from his dream, but he couldn't think of what it was. They ate in silence for a while.

Then Jesse remembered what he had meant to say the night before. Samar had insisted on silence during their trek to the oasis. "Thank you for coming back yesterday."

Silas just nodded. "I don't leave squad members behind."

Rae didn't chime in with a compliment, but she wasn't scowling either. Jesse took that as an agreement.

Wait. Silas' words repeated in Jesse's mind. *"I don't leave squad members behind."*

All of a sudden, the images of his dream came bursting back into Jesse's memory. Captain Demetri's face from behind the bars of the prison, talking. *Your friends must be prepared to reap the whirlwind they released.* Darkness. Shouting. *Why were there only two Guard members in your party?* The dull clang of metal. Captain Demetri on the ground, eyes closed. Still breathing.

"Parvel," Jesse said tonelessly. He looked up at Rae and Silas. "What about Parvel?"

"We'll go back for him, of course," Silas said, shrugging. "He will know what to do next. He always does."

"No, you don't understand," Jesse blurted, standing. "We have to go *now*. Before *he* gets there. Except he might have already left."

Both of them were staring at him now. "Jesse, you're not making any sense," Rae said bluntly. "Calm down and explain."

"Captain Demetri," Jesse said miserably. "I told him where Parvel was. Since we got away, where do you think he'll go next?"

"To Mir," Silas said, his face as hard as stone. "To find Parvel. I should have killed that captain when I had the chance."

That was my fault too, Jesse realized, his heart sinking. *Parvel could die because of me.*

"Why did you tell him?" Rae demanded. "Didn't you think…?"

"He said they'd torture you if I didn't answer!"

"You didn't have to give him the name of the village. Did you draw him a map while you were at it?"

"Enough!" Silas exclaimed. Rae folded her arms sullenly. "We can't change what has already happened. We can only go forward, as quickly as we can."

None questioned whether or not they would go back for Parvel. They couldn't abandon him to die. Jesse had to admit to himself that the idea of returning home, even if it was just for a brief time, appealed to him. "When do we leave?" he asked.

"Leave?" a voice asked. "Why, you just got here!"

They turned to see Samar, crossing his arms and frowning down at them. "It would be rude to abandon your host so soon," he warned sternly.

Silas began to stammer out an apologetic explanation when Samar grinned. "No, young Amarian, I understand. You must do what you must. I will have my three best camels saddled immediately. With supplies, of course."

"And you?" Jesse asked the old man. "What will you do?"

Samar sighed. "I will stay in Asher, the village near this oasis," he said. "It is the village where my father met my mother, you know. It was where I was born. It is where I will die. As they say in Da'armos, '*Karde de'larsih.*' Life is a circle."

"We are sorry to go so soon," Jesse said, standing from his mat. Rae and Silas followed.

"Think nothing of it," Samar said, shaking his head. He began to scurry off through the camp to gather their supplies. Jesse, Silas, and Rae followed.

"We are grateful for all you've done for us," Silas said, "and for the kingdom."

"Oh!" Samar said, stopping so suddenly Jesse nearly fell into him. "I nearly forgot! You are Youth Guard!"

"Yes," Rae said slowly, looking at Samar as if he had been out too long in the desert heat. "We already told you that."

"No, no," Samar said impatiently. "That's not what I mean. It's about your mission."

Without realizing it, all of them leaned forward slightly. "In all the confusion, it had slipped my mind," Samar continued, shaking his head at his forgetfulness. "I meant to tell you in the tunnel, but we had to keep silent and—"

"Just tell us!" Rae burst out.

Samar gave her a scolding look for her outburst. "Patience, young one." He cleared his throat. "What I wanted to tell you was that while you were being held in the dungeon at Da'ra, I asked some questions for you about the obidhala and Amarias' relationship with Da'armos. What I learned was quite surprising."

He paused, and now it was Jesse's turn to bite back impatient words. "About the obidhala?" he prompted.

Samar shook his head. "No. About the payment of tribute to Amarias." He gave the three Youth Guard members a confused look. "Jesse, the Sheik sent this year's tribute to Amarias a month ago."

"What?" Silas exclaimed. This was interesting news indeed. "But why...?" His voice trailed off as he glanced at Jesse and Rae.

"Every coin of the tribute was sent to the capital of District Four, Leden," Samar said. "I talked with the one who led the caravan to deliver it."

"Was he a smuggler too?" Rae asked, raising a skeptical eyebrow. It was a good point.

"This one happened to be a she," Samar acknowledged, "but, as to your question, I have no doubt that a few silver coins disappeared from the load along the way. But she swore that the rest arrived at the governor's palace there. I trust her word."

So our entire mission was pointless, meant to have us killed, just as Captain Demetri said.

"But why would your king send you to collect a tribute he had already received?" Samar questioned, stroking his beard. "Especially at great risk to your lives?"

"That" Silas said grimly, "is why we have to leave."

It seemed to be answer enough to Samar, who dragged Silas away. "Come, young Amarian. You must help me saddle the camels." Samar bustled through the camp, shouting orders to his servants for more water skins, checking to make sure the saddles were cinched tight and the weight evenly distributed.

I will miss him, Jesse realized, watching the old man with a smile.

When he turned to Rae, she was gone. Somehow she had climbed up the nearby sand dune without Jesse noticing. She simply stood there, watching the sun sink lower in the sky.

For some reason, Jesse felt like he should join her. He dragged himself up the dune and stood next to her for a few minutes.

Rae was the first to break the silence. "We didn't complete our mission," she said, still looking out at the desert.

Jesse stared at her in disbelief. "Rae, the king's Patrol *and* the Da'armon guards were trying to kill us. The very fact that we escaped alive is a miracle."

"I hate running," Rae said, clenching her fists. "We ran from the assassins, then we ran out of Da'ra, and now we're running again. Why can't we just stay and fight?"

The answer seemed fairly simple to Jesse. "Because we'd die."

Rae sighed loudly. "It still seems cowardly to me."

"It's not," Jesse said. "It's just being smart. We can't save Parvel if we're dead."

"I suppose not," Rae said, turning to him for the first time. She didn't look convinced. "This is not what I had planned when I joined the Guard."

"Silas and I will keep us alive," Jesse said, shrugging. "You can keep us fighting. That's important too."

"Even if we're fighting against the king?" Rae pointed out.

"Especially then," Jesse said. "Because, let me tell you, I'm going to want to give up, probably a hundred times, before we get back to Parvel. But you can't let me."

She smiled a little at that. "That's right. We're Youth Guard. We don't give up until our quest is complete."

Jesse liked the way she said "we."

"Come on," she said, hurrying back to the camp. "We can't let Silas leave without us. He'd probably get lost in the desert again."

Silas had their camels ready, and once Samar instructed them about their route several times, he bowed to them.

"If you should ever need me," he said, "I will be here, ready to do what I can." His eyes glinted with laughter. "But, if you can manage not to be chased by Amarian assassins or thrown into a Da'armon dungeon again, I would appreciate it. I have seen enough adventure in my years."

Silas laughed. "I should hope we wouldn't go through all that again." He prodded his camel forward—as usual, leading the way. "Thank you for all you have done, Samariyosin," he called back.

Before Jesse joined his friends, he turned to Samar. "You saved our lives many times," he began.

Samar waved his thanks away with a shake of his old, withered hand. "Don't thank me, Jesse. Thank the One who numbers the stars."

"Perhaps it was just a coincidence," Jesse suggested, only half believing the explanation himself.

Samar shook his head. "No. He listened to me, Jesse. I know it. And now, even if it takes the rest of my days, I will listen for Him too, and I will find Him."

There was nothing Jesse could say to that. The old man, once lonely and worn, looked content, his wrinkled face smiling peacefully.

"I wish we had something to give you to show our thanks," Jesse said.

"*Ta'el ashid*," Samar said in reply. "We all have stories." He nodded at Jesse. "You listened to my story, then became a part of it. It is enough."

Jesse nodded and smiled at the old man. "Good-bye, Samar."

"Good-bye, Jesse."

Before his camel lurched over the dunes, Jesse turned to wave at his friend. But Samar was already gone, gesturing wildly as he hurried to complete the next task that demanded his attention.

Maybe Parvel was right, Jesse thought to himself, adjusting to the swaying rhythm of the camel's movements. *Maybe there is a God after all.* It was a thought worth considering.

If you're there, Jesse found himself praying, *and if you listen to people like me, please let us get to Parvel before Captain Demetri.* They could not leave Parvel behind. Jesse had promised, and he intended to keep his promise.

The sun, just dipping down in the sky, was not as hot as it had been while they slept in the afternoon. It was a good time to leave, Jesse knew. *A good time to go home.*

CHAPTER 18

Demetri stumbled toward the gates of Nalatid. He had traveled for days through the desert, stopping only for a few hours of sleep before continuing on. The Guard Rider medallion around his neck seemed to burn against him, as if it knew he had failed.

It was not my fault, he wanted to shout. *I did not mean for them to escape.* After all his careful planning, to be outwitted by mere children—it was humiliating. But who could have predicted their disappearance from the smuggler's caravan? Or the swarm of kaltharas at the execution? Or a girl dropping down from a clothesline?

Demetri could not understand it. The way everything had worked out so perfectly for them was impossible. Not miraculous, of course, just odd-defying luck. He had supervised the search of the city. They had issued a large reward, ransacked every house in every district, and tightly sealed all of the gates...but still no sign of the Youth Guard members or their smuggler friends. It was as if they had simply disappeared.

More importantly, the crippled one, the one who was not of the Guard at all, knew the truth. He knew—Demetri had told him—that the king wanted to kill all Youth Guard members. That knowledge would make them much harder to find and trap the next time.

If there was a next time. Aleric did not seem to be the forgiving type. Demetri knew Aleric would follow through with his threat to kill his brother. As for how he would know about Demetri's failure….

He is watching. Somehow, he will find out. Demetri had never been one for idle superstitions, but he was sure of this. Perhaps Aleric had sent a spy to follow him, or had heard of his failure by some other means, but there was no doubt in Demetri's mind that he knew. It was not a suspicion or a prediction, but a fact, as neat and simple as the ones he recorded in his books.

It was nearly dusk when Demetri stumbled through the streets of Nalatid. Several of his Patrol members saluted as he passed, but he did not acknowledge any of them. He shut himself into his quarters and locked the door, collapsing on his bed without even taking off his uniform.

He did not want to go to sleep. Ever since Aleric had given him the medallion, the nightmares had gotten worse. The deeper the sleep, the more vivid the memories. They were always the painful memories, the ones he had tried the hardest to forget. And they always ended with the night of the betrayal.

Demetri's body was exhausted from traveling long nights with no rest. His eyes closed, shutting out the world.

He was in the desert at night—the nightmares were always in the desert. But this time, instead of his Youth Guard squad, Aleric stepped out of the darkness.

Although Demetri knew he should be surprised to see him, he was not. It was almost as if he had been waiting for him.

"You let them go," Aleric said simply. His pale eyes seemed to glow like twin moons.

Demetri nodded, taking the full blame without making excuses, as a soldier should. "Then you know what happened."

Aleric nodded. "I saw it all."

"How can that be?" But even as he asked, Demetri felt his hand go to the Youth Guard medallion around his neck. He pulled it from beneath his clothes. In the darkness, the symbol of the king seemed to glow with a faint red light. He held it out, staring at it, until Aleric's voice jerked his gaze away.

"You know what you must do," Aleric said.

It surprised Demetri that he did. It was as clear as if the plan had been written in the sand in front of him. "I will go to Mir and kill the squad member they left behind."

"Yes," Aleric said. "The squad captain, fallen to poison."

"Most likely the work of the Rebellion," Demetri decided.

"Yes, we often find them our most helpful allies. They think, as everyone else does that the king depends on the Youth Guard. Of course, members of the Rebellion seek to stop them whenever possible. Sometimes they even save us the job of killing them." Aleric chuckled. "I love irony."

"I will kill the others when they return to their captain," Demetri continued. "I simply have to get to Mir before they do. I am sure they will come. They refuse to leave each other behind, even at the risk of their own lives."

Aleric nodded, a glint of cruelty flashing in his eyes. "A kind of loyalty you know nothing about, if I remember correctly, Captain."

With a cry that came from deep inside him, Demetri lunged forward and put his hands around Aleric's throat. "Do not say that" he said, in a low, deadly tone. "I did not mean to betray them."

"Let me go," Aleric gasped, fighting for breath. "Would you betray your brother too?"

Demetri dropped him in disgust. He hated the power Aleric had over him. *Maybe it would have been better if I had died with my squad in the desert five years ago.* It was not the first time he'd had that thought.

"Put the medallion back on," Aleric commanded.

Somehow, the medallion had fallen on the ground. Demetri had not even remembered taking it off. He replaced it, and immediately felt calmer, more focused. "Why me?" Demetri said flatly. "Why would you even want me?"

"Because you have something that none of our other Riders have," Aleric said simply, never looking away. "Most are thoroughly consumed with gaining power, but you are different. You have love. Love for your friends, who you unknowingly betrayed to their deaths, and now love for your brother."

My brother. Demetri straightened out of his slump, pulling his shoulders and head up. He could feel the anger in his eyes, flashing like the emerald eyes of a hungry dragon. "I will join you," he said, bowing to Aleric. "I will find the three, and they will get what they deserve."

"A powerful statement indeed," Aleric said. "And I believe you."

Once more, Demetri felt the old man's eyes boring into him, and once more Demetri was the first to look away. "Do not fail us again."

With that he disappeared, blending into the growing night, like he was a part of the darkness. *And maybe he is.*

A thunderclap seemed to tear the desert in two with a streak of lightning so bright Demetri fell facedown in the sand, cowering to get away from the brightness. For a moment, over the thunder, he thought he heard someone screaming.

With a start, Demetri awoke. The sun was pouring through the window. He would have to hurry to get to Mir before the Youth Guard members. It would be a long journey.

He felt under his uniform. The medallion was still there. It seemed to give Demetri strength, a power he had never known before, and he knew that this time, he would not fail.

J'abbet ses mitren, oldrivar lakita ses omidreden. The whirlwind had been unleashed. It had taken hundreds of the Youth Guard over the decades. It had taken Demetri's friends five years before. It would soon take the three Guard members.

It had even, in some way, taken the person Demetri had once been.

But it would not take the new Captain Demetri. It would not take Aleric. They and those like them would be standing when the wind died down and the dust cleared.

And the rest? They, like the Youth Guard members, would die.